"Did you see who was shooting at you?" Peyton twisted her hands together and drew a ragged breath.

"I didn't see anyone." Colin coaxed her hands apart and held them in his. "Try not to worry. We'll find out soon enough who was out there."

The sirens were louder now, probably a few hundred yards from the driveway. She turned the pistol around and offered it to him. "You'd better take this. If the cops see a Sterling with a gun, they'll probably shoot first and ask questions later."

"I think you're doing Gatlinburg PD a disservice in thinking that. But I understand where you're coming from." He shoved the pistol into his waistband, then cupped her face between his hands.

Her silver-gray eyes caught the moonlight as she stared at him in surprise.

He shouldn't kiss her. It would be a mistake on so many levels. But he also knew there was no way he could *not* kiss her at that moment.

CONFLICTING EVIDENCE

LENA DIAZ

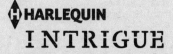

To George, for encouraging me to dream with my eyes wide open.
Love you, babe.

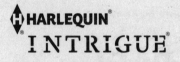

**Recycling programs
for this product may
not exist in your area.**

ISBN-13: 978-1-335-13629-9

Conflicting Evidence

Copyright © 2020 by Lena Diaz

This edition published by arrangement with Harlequin Books S.A.

For questions and comments about the quality of this book,
please contact us at CustomerService@Harlequin.com.

Harlequin Enterprises ULC
22 Adelaide St. West, 40th Floor
Toronto, Ontario M5H 4E3, Canada
www.Harlequin.com

Printed in U.S.A.

Lena Diaz was born in Kentucky and has also lived in California, Louisiana and Florida, where she now resides with her husband and two children. Before becoming a romantic suspense author, she was a computer programmer. A Romance Writers of America Golden Heart® Award finalist, she has also won the prestigious Daphne du Maurier Award for Excellence in Mystery/Suspense. To get the latest news about Lena, please visit her website, lenadiaz.com.

Visit the Author Profile page at Harlequin.com.

CAST OF CHARACTERS

Colin McKenzie—This deputy US marshal nearly lost his life in an arsonist's fire. But when his testimony sent the firebug away, Colin lost his fiancée. Peyton couldn't forgive him for sending her brother to prison.

Peyton Sterling—Peyton's brother has escaped and she must face her past all over again—the brother whom she fiercely believes is innocent, and the man she's never stopped loving.

Brian Sterling—He went to prison for a fire that left Colin McKenzie in a burn unit. Was he really guilty? Or has he been paying for someone else's crimes all along?

Benjamin Sterling—Reputation is everything to Peyton and Brian's father. When Brian escapes prison, Ben desperately wants him caught. Is he trying to save face, or is he trying to save someone else—again?

Joan Fairmont—Kindhearted Peyton gives Joan a second chance by hiring her in spite of Joan's criminal past. Is Joan paying back Peyton's kindness with a brand of evil all her own?

Damon Patterson—This convicted murderer orchestrated the prison escape. Is he setting fires and framing Brian? Or is Brian using him as a fall guy?

Chapter One

Fresh shoe prints in the dirt outside the abandoned Sterling homestead confirmed that Deputy US Marshal Colin McKenzie's hunch was likely right—the arsonist who'd nearly destroyed Colin's life a decade ago was back. And once again, Colin was going to put Brian Sterling right where he belonged—in prison.

But he had to catch him first.

He drew his Glock 22 and scanned the thick woods that surrounded this remote mountain property half an hour southwest of Gatlinburg, Tennessee. Late-afternoon sun slanted across the one-story craftsman-style house, casting shadows along the sagging porch. The once proud structure sported peeling yellowed paint that had started out white, railings missing most of their spindles and a cracked picture window that he remembered had an amazing view of the Smoky Mountains.

Back when the Sterling siblings and the McKenzie brothers had gone to Gatlinburg–Pittman High School together, a split three-rail fence had marked the line where a manicured lawn ended and wilderness began. Now, half the posts were tipping like drunks desperately trying to catch their balance. The rest littered the ground, having surrendered to the high winds and violent storms that often blew through the area. This decaying family home was a sad reminder of what the Sterlings had lost, all because of the selfish son who'd destroyed everyone's plans for the future.

Including Colin's.

He tightened his grip on his gun and crouched down to make himself less of a target as he crept from the gravel driveway to the house. Most of the windows didn't have curtains or even blinds anymore, giving him a decent view of the rooms. They were surprisingly neat and tidy. Maybe the Sterlings paid someone to come up from town every few months to clean the place. Too bad they weren't paying equal attention to the outside.

After a full circuit around the structure, he was confident his nemesis wasn't inside waiting to take a shot at him. A tour of the cobweb-filled shed and the sadly empty horse barn out back confirmed that no one had been in them for quite some time, probably years.

Cursing the summer heat, he wiped a bead of sweat from his forehead and returned to the front yard. All the while, he kept his pistol trained on the trees that surrounded the property. Was Brian out there right now, watching him? Or had someone else left that shoe print?

It wasn't like a hiker would accidentally stumble across this place. The Great Smoky Mountains National Park and the Appalachian Trail were several rugged miles east. And the steep winding road up here only led to the Sterling homestead and one other house, Colin's, two miles farther up the mountain. But Brian didn't know that. Colin had purchased the land and built his home several years after the Sterlings left Gatlinburg for Memphis.

From what Colin had heard, the move cost Brian's father over half his client list. Had he been able to rehabilitate his once successful financial-advisor career in Memphis? Did his wife find a church community that she enjoyed as much as the one here? Was their daughter happy? Had she managed to forget everyone here she'd once loved, or who'd once loved her?

Colin tightened his grip on his pistol.

He didn't have the answers to any of those questions. All he knew for sure was that the family had sacrificed everything to move six hours away so they could be closer to FCI, the Federal Correctional Institution, where Brian was serving his fifteen-year sentence.

Until he'd decided to give himself a get-out-of-jail-early card less than twenty-four hours ago.

Colin hadn't seriously expected that the escaped convict would risk the long drive to Gatlinburg with his face plastered all over the news. But Brian wasn't known for being a deep thinker. He wasn't known for thinking much about his actions at all, or their impact on others. At nineteen he'd nearly burned two people alive. Now, at twenty-nine, while escaping a prison transport van that was taking him to the courthouse, he'd murdered a police officer. He'd made a wife a widow, a young son fatherless and put a target on his back for the entire Tennessee law-enforcement community.

Without noticing any movement near the tree line, and hearing only the sound of his own boots crunching on dry weeds and gravel, Colin eased back to his pickup. A few minutes later, he concealed his truck behind a stand of basswood trees about thirty feet from the roadway. Hoofing it from there, he selected a heavily canopied oak that would offer a clear view of the house while providing him with shade and concealment. After settling onto a thick branch a third of the way up the tree, he leaned back against the trunk and stretched out his long legs in front of him. Now, all he had to do was wait.

Chapter Two

Peyton Sterling coaxed her aging SUV up the long bumpy driveway that was more dirt than gravel. Her home loomed ahead and she immediately averted her gaze.

Focus on the garage. Don't look at the rest of the house. Don't look at the house.

But, of course, she did, and winced. Even though it had been over three months since she'd returned to Gatlinburg, the sight of her mom's weed-choked flower beds and the dilapidated family home still made her heart ache.

The life insurance money and small inheritance that she'd received had gotten her through so far. She'd paid a repairman to do the bare minimum to make it functional, like install a new garage door opener because she could barely lift the door otherwise. And she'd had no choice but to use a chunk of the money to renovate the kitchen. That was a necessity for her fledgling business, an investment in her future. Unfortunately, fixing everything else that was wrong with the house wasn't an expense that she could justify, or afford. Fixing them herself wasn't feasible either. She was far from handy in the home improvement department. If she tried to repair a leaky faucet she'd probably end up flooding the entire house.

Of course, even if she'd been handy, by the time she got home every evening, she was too tired to do much more than grab a bite to eat before collapsing into bed. Then she had to be up before dawn to bake fresh delicacies for the café and start the whole cycle all over again. There wasn't enough time, energy or money to make a dent in her long to-do list at home.

Thankfully, tomorrow was Saturday, the one day of the week when she had two full-time helpers at the shop instead of just one. With Joan and Melissa taking care of things, she could sleep in. But it wasn't like she could relax and do nothing all day. She had to use her day off to catch up on laundry, clean the house, work on the books for the store, order new supplies. In some ways, she worked harder on her "day off" than during the rest of the week.

Blowing out a deep breath, she parked inside the garage and then forced her tired body out of the SUV. If an aching back and bruised-feeling feet were what it took to make a business profitable, Peyton's Place should have been a roaring success by now. Unfortunately, success was coming much more slowly than she'd hoped. Sometimes the only thing keeping her from quitting was the worry over where Melissa and Joan would end up if she had to close the shop's doors.

After slapping her palm on the garage door button on the wall, she headed into the mudroom. As always, when she continued into the kitchen, the creamy yellow walls and white shaker-style cabinets embraced her like a hug, helping to ease the tension that had built up in her shoulders all day. This was her domain. This was where she felt most at home. And it was one of the few things that could always make her smile.

She hung her purse on a peg beside the door. But instead of heading through the cased opening on the left into the family room, she smoothed her hand over the cool marble island. If she was honest with herself, renovating the kitchen and bringing it into the current century wasn't just to enable her to supply her café with fresh baked goods. It fed her soul as well.

The sinfully luxurious stainless-steel Sub-Zero refrigerator, the double ovens built into the wall, the high-end finishes helped make this room her happy place. The treasured memories within these walls were priceless. Especially now.

I miss you so much, Mom.

Her father had labeled her and her mother obsessed. Maybe they had been. But there was no denying that her happiest memories revolved around cooking. Either they'd been making s'mores in the family room fireplace or she and her mom had been in here baking cakes, cookies and pastries. Somehow, kneading dough or making frosting from scratch could help Peyton forget the arguments, the trouble her brother kept getting into, even her mother's eccentric tendencies and unpredictable mood swings. When Peyton was working in the kitchen, all her troubles seemed to melt away.

Even now, just smelling a loaf of bread baking in the oven could transport her back to her high school days, when she was young and in love, happier than she'd ever been and probably ever would be again. To a time when her family was relatively whole, when *she* was still whole. But those days were gone and could never be recaptured. One horrific event had fragmented their lives forever. She'd lost everything that mattered that night. Or, at least, that's what she'd thought, until a slippery, rainy road just a few months ago proved she'd still had more to lose.

I love you, Mom. Wish you were here.

Her shoulders slumped as she reluctantly turned from her homey, comforting kitchen toward the opening to the family room. She needed to head to her bedroom, shower, change into her pajamas. But just looking at the cave-like gloom beyond the doorway was already making her feel down. Had it always been that dark? Or did it just seem that way now that the family who'd once lived in this place no longer existed? The only warm body around here at the moment was Peyton. Unless she counted the rats and squirrels that had taken up residence after she and her parents moved to Memphis.

She'd lost count of how many critters she'd either chased out or carried out after setting traps. Based on the scratching sounds she sometimes still heard in the walls, there were a few stubborn holdouts she'd yet to evict. Squeezing her eyes shut, she tried to recapture her earlier contentment. Remember the scent of all those candles her mom used to set around the house on evenings when it was too hot to light a fire in the fireplace. She could almost picture it, see her mom's sweet smile, hear the rustle of fabric as her mom put on a crisp white apron.

"Hey, Peyton."

Her eyes flew open. She automatically grabbed the

broom that she always kept propped against the wall just in case another rat made an appearance. But she froze when a painfully thin man with strawberry blond hair a shade darker than hers emerged from the shadows to stand in the kitchen opening. Her jaw dropped open in shock as he watched her, his sheepish grin not quite reaching his haunted eyes.

"Long time, no see, huh, sis?"

"B…Brian?" Her voice came out a choked whisper as she struggled to make sense of what she was seeing. Of *who* she was seeing. "I don't understand. Is that really you?"

A sound behind her had her whirling around to see another man emerge from the laundry room. She pressed a shaking hand to her throat as she drank in the achingly familiar short dark hair, shoulders that had broadened and filled out since she'd last seen him. He was taller now too, towering over her, making the kitchen seem much smaller than it had moments ago.

He was dressed in light gray pants, a white button-up shirt and a tie. His sleeves were long in spite of the warm temperatures outside. Little white scars on the backs of his hands left no doubt about the reason for those long sleeves. Her heart seemed to stutter in her chest and her throat tightened.

"Colin?" The once treasured name that she hadn't allowed past her lips in years tumbled from them in a whisper that was a dash of pain and a huge dollop of guilt.

He didn't even glance at her.

He slid a pistol out of the holster on his hip and leveled it at her brother. "Brian Sterling, you're under arrest for felony escape and the murder of Officer Owen Jennings."

Peyton drew in a sharp breath. What was Colin talking about? He was arresting her brother? Dear God, no. This couldn't be happening. Not again.

The blood seemed to drain from her brother's face, leaving him a gaunt, frightened shadow of the person he used to be. His haunted gray eyes, the same ones that Peyton saw every time she looked in a mirror, pleaded with her to help him. The same eyes that had stared at her in bewilderment from the back seat of a squad car as a barn burned to the ground in the distance. The same ones that had blurred with tears on the other side of a thick glass partition in the prison's visiting room when Peyton broke the news about their mother's death.

She stood frozen, the broom clutched in her hand. It was ten years ago all over again. And just like then, she was forced to make a choice that no one should ever have to make—the choice between the man she loved and her own flesh and blood.

She slammed the broom against Colin's forearm, knocking the pistol out of his hand.

"Run, Brian! Run!" she choked out.

He whirled around and took off toward the front door.

Colin swiped his pistol up off the hardwood floor and gave her a furious, searing look that burned right through her heart. Then he sprinted through the house after her brother.

Chapter Three

Peyton twisted her hands together in her lap as she sat beside one of the desks in the squad room, waiting to discover her fate. The police officer who'd ordered her to sit there was talking to a handful of other men and women at the far end of the vast, open room. It seemed like every cop in Gatlinburg was here. The place was buzzing with anger and excitement as they studied maps and gathered flashlights, preparing to hunt her brother down like a rabid dog.

She wanted to scream, shake them, somehow make them realize what she couldn't all those years ago: *her brother was innocent.* The only thing stopping her was that there was no denying what she'd seen with her own eyes—Brian, standing in her kitchen five years before his sentence was up. They were right that he'd broken out of prison. But they were wrong about the horrible, evil thing they also claimed that he'd done—killed a Memphis police officer after the escape.

Brian had always been headstrong and rebellious, with anger and impulse-control issues that had had him seeing a therapist from the time he was ten years old. But he was also sweet and sensitive. Never a bully, he was the kid who got picked on by his classmates because he was so awkward and shy. He adored animals and had gotten in trouble countless times for bringing home strays. The brother who cried after watching a sad commercial could never have set fire to a building with two people inside. That was the reason she could never, ever believe in his guilt. And that was the reason she knew that he hadn't shot that police officer in Memphis.

"Is that why you came back to Gatlinburg? Because you knew your brother was planning to escape and you wanted to be here to help him?"

She jerked around to meet Colin McKenzie's accusing stare as he stood beside the desk. It pained her that his deep voice, angry or not, sent the same jolt of longing through her that it had since they'd both turned fifteen and discovered their friendship had blossomed into something more. The cute boy who'd made all the girls' hearts flutter in high school had matured into a mouth-wateringly gorgeous man. But all that physical perfection was spoiled by the look of hate blazing from his stormy blue eyes.

The hate was definitely new.

"I suppose from your viewpoint I deserve that. But, no. Why I came back has nothing to do with my brother. Even though he was wrongfully convicted, I would never help him escape from prison."

"You'd just help him escape from your kitchen when a law-enforcement officer placed him under arrest. Is that the line you've drawn in the sand?"

She curled her fingers against her palms. "Okay, I *definitely* deserved that. And I completely understand that it looked that way to you. But from my viewpoint, my *innocent* brother was being threatened with a gun. I was protecting him."

He jerked his shirt sleeve up a few inches on his left arm, revealing a smattering of puckered burn scars. "I pulled two people out of a burning barn after your brother set the fire. *Innocent* isn't a word I'd use to describe him."

Threatening tears burned her eyes but she viciously held them back. "I'm sorry, Colin. About everything. I truly am. I hate that you were hurt. But the truth hasn't changed. Brian didn't set that fire."

He jerked his sleeve back down. "Do you *want* to go to prison?"

She stared at him in surprise. "What?"

"You're in a precarious position, Peyton. If I officially arrest you and the DA decides to press charges, you could end up in prison for aiding and abetting a felon."

"But, I didn't mean—"

"Why did you do it? Why did you help him?"

She spread her hands in a helpless gesture. "I told you. I was protecting him. It was instinct. A choice—family or..." She chewed her lip.

"Or me. And once again, you didn't choose me."

The bitterness in his voice made her ache. But there was nothing she could do, nothing she could say that could ever fix what she'd destroyed so many years ago.

Because he was right.

"Give me a reason *not* to arrest you."

She slowly shook her head, no longer able to hold back the tears. "I can't. What I did today was wrong. I know that. But it was automatic, without any rational thought behind it. I'd probably do the same thing again if I had a do-over. Protecting my family is as ingrained in me as breathing. Can't you understand that?"

Every muscle in his body seemed to tense, as if he was debating what to say but didn't trust himself to speak.

She brushed the tears from her cheeks.

He swore softly and turned away, his ground-eating stride quickly taking him across the room to one of the groups of officers talking by a window.

Sniffing, she breathed deeply, willing the tears to stop. And all the while, she watched him, unable to look away. Her gaze caressed his profile the way her fingers once had. She knew every angle of his chiseled face, had traced the stubble across his jaw to his hairline, had kissed the barely there mustache. He still maintained that same look, like a man who hadn't shaved in three days. But where she'd loved and adored the boy, she didn't know what to make of the man. He was a stranger, with the power to destroy the fragile new world she'd created. And she couldn't even give him a reason not to.

He nodded at something one of the men said, then strode back to the desk. "Get up."

Her face flushed hot with embarrassment. She stood and smoothed her jeans and blouse into place before holding her wrists out in front of her.

He frowned. "What are you doing?"

"Hoping you won't make me put my hands behind my back to put the handcuffs on. This is humiliating enough as it is." When he only stared at her, she lowered her arms. "Aren't you arresting me?"

"That depends on whether you'll give me what I want."

She drew in a sharp breath, his words awakening memories of the two of them together. His mouth, hot against her neck. His tongue tracing the valley between her breasts. His teasing smile as he slid down her body and hooked his fingers into the top of her jeans.

His breath hitched. "Don't look at me that way, Peyton."

She shivered and ruthlessly fought back the erotic images that had goose bumps breaking out all over her suddenly hypersensitive skin. Trying to pretend ignorance, she asked, "What do you mean?"

His eyes narrowed. "Like you're remembering how good it was between us."

She swallowed, remembering exactly how good it had been.

His blue eyes darkened, but not with passion. "The past, what you and I shared, died the day you left Gatlinburg without so much as a goodbye. A lifetime of growing up together, four years of dating, of sharing everything two people supposedly in love can share, and you couldn't bring yourself to answer any of my calls, respond to even one of my texts. Well I got the message from you, loud and clear. And nothing could ever make me go down that road again."

Her face flamed at his cruel, unnecessary rejection. She cast a surreptitious glance around the room before sinking back down into the chair so she could put some space between the two of them. Thankfully, no one seemed to be paying any attention to her and Colin at the moment. They were all too busy making plans to go after her only sibling.

Wait. Phone calls? Texts? What was he talking about? He'd never called her, not once. "Colin, I don't understand. What are you—"

"What I want is to make a deal with you. Your co-operation in exchange for your brother's life."

She pressed a hand against her throat, unable to reconcile his shocking words with the man standing before her. This wasn't the Colin she remembered, not even close. Had she ever really known him at all? Or was this hard, unyielding man the result of what *she'd* done?

"You're seriously threatening to kill him if I don't cooperate? How could you be so heartless and cruel?"

His eyes narrowed again, his brow wrinkling with anger. "Don't accuse me of contemplating murder as if you have some moral high ground to stand on."

She gasped with outrage. But before she could respond, he leaned toward her, arms braced on the desk, crowding her back against her chair.

"Unlike your cop-killing brother," he said in a furious whisper, "I'm not a murderer. I wasn't saying that I was going to harm Brian. Look around you, Peyton. *I'm* not the threat. *Everyone else* is. They're all fired up to hunt him down. Once the trackers get here, his chances plummet to near zero."

Alarm skittered up her spine. "Trackers? Chances? What are you saying?"

"Your brother murdered a law-enforcement officer. He—"

"No. He didn't. He wouldn't."

Colin made a frustrated sound in his throat before

grabbing a chair from beside a nearby desk and rolling it in front of her. He plopped down and moved close, his knees almost touching hers.

"They're bringing in bloodhounds to hunt down your brother and the other escapees." He kept his voice low, barely above a whisper. "Police officers and federal agents are lining up in neighboring counties, demanding a chance to help with the search. They're going to find them, Peyton. A cop killer isn't going to escape, not around here."

"Stop saying that. My brother's not a killer." She let out a ragged breath. "Please, Colin. Stop."

Something shifted behind his eyes, like clouds tumbling through a darkening sky. He drew a slow, deep breath and glanced around the room as if to get himself under control. When he looked at her again, some of the anger seemed to have drained out of him. In its place was a sense of urgency and frustration, visible in the tense set of his shoulders, the firm line of his jaw.

"What I'm trying to tell you is that Brian's life is in danger. Not because anyone is going to purposely try to kill him. But because everyone is hyperaware that someone who's shot one police officer won't hesitate to pull the trigger on another."

"But—"

He held a hand up to stop her. "What you don't seem to understand is that whether or not Brian's the one who pulled the trigger doesn't matter. The officer was killed when Brian and three other criminals escaped. Under the law, all four of them are guilty of felony murder."

Muscle memory had her reaching for his hand before she even thought about what she was doing. To her surprise, he took it, and entwined their fingers together. In spite of his anger, in spite of everything that had happened, or maybe because of it, Colin McKenzie was holding her hand. And just like that, she was able to pick up the pieces of her crumbling world and glue them back together.

It had always been that way between them. A simple look, or the warmth of his touch, grounded her, calmed her when things were going wrong. How odd that it would work today when he was part of the reason that her world was falling apart.

"What does felony murder mean exactly?" she whispered, barely able to force the words past her tight throat. "Does it mean…does it mean Brian could face the death penalty?"

He nodded, his hand tightening around hers.

"Oh, dear Lord. What am I going to do?"

"All you *can* do for now is help me try to save his life. Worry about the trial, about possible penalties, later. The entire law-enforcement community is on edge. They feel like their uniforms make them a target for a man who's already killed one of their own. They'll be quicker than normal to pull the trigger, out of self-preservation. That makes for an exceedingly dangerous situation, all the way around."

His words rang true. The room was bursting with anger, nervous energy. Soon they'd be searching for her brother with that dangerous mix of emotions fueled by fear and adrenaline, while heavily armed. Brian was in a world of trouble, even worse than she'd realized.

"What kind of a deal are you offering?"

"I won't lie and pretend that I can guarantee your

brother's safety. But he has a better chance of making it out of the mountains alive if I'm the one who catches him."

She blinked. "You? But you…"

"Have more reason than most to want to catch him? You've got that right. But out of respect for your parents, whom I once thought of as my own family, I'd like to capture their son alive and give him a chance in the courts instead of against a hail of bullets. If you cooperate fully, help me figure out where he might be hiding, then I'll hold off on arresting you for now."

His implied threat had her tugging her hand free. "Hold off? For now? What does that mean?"

He flexed his fingers and sat back, his face an unreadable mask. "I reserve the right to arrest you and charge you with a felony for that stunt you pulled at your family's house today. If you don't legitimately help me figure out where he is, I *will* put you in jail and bring you up on charges."

"You're forcing me to choose again? Between you and my brother?"

He arched a brow. "What would be the point? We both know how that would turn out."

She jerked back, his words stabbing her like a hundred daggers straight to the heart. But it wasn't the words that hurt the most. It was the pain that leached through his tone, pain he was obviously trying to hide beneath a veil of rage. His pain was so much worse to bear than his fury, because she was the one who'd caused it. She'd taken a sweet, kind young man and twisted him into this bitter, angry person in front of her.

She wrapped her arms around her middle and closed

her eyes, shutting out the ugliness of everything that had happened, everything that was still happening. Somehow, she had to get a handle on her swirling emotions, without relying on her former childhood sweetheart to help her. She had to find the inner strength to do this on her own. If she gave in to her emotions, she'd slide onto the floor in a boneless puddle of anguish and self-disgust. And that wouldn't help anyone.

"Peyton?" His voice was laced with impatience now. *Breathe. Just breathe. Pull yourself together.*

"Peyton? Are you okay? Do I need to call an EMT?"

The genuine concern underlying his tone had her eyes fluttering open. The truth was there, in the way he was watching her so intently. In spite of everything, he still cared. Maybe she hadn't destroyed him after all. Maybe there was still some goodness left inside. Maybe, just maybe, she could trust him to help Brian.

She straightened, drew a bracing breath. "No, I'm… I'll be okay. Thank you."

He frowned, seemingly unconvinced. But he gave her a curt nod and motioned toward the groups of officers scattered around the room. "You can play the odds and wait and see if the makeshift posse shoots first and asks questions later. Or you can work with me to increase his odds of being brought in alive. That's the offer that I'm making. It's your choice. But you have to make a decision. Right now."

"What happens if I say yes, that I'll try to help you?"

"Since your house is still being processed as a crime scene, we go back to my place and you answer my questions there. You tell me everything he's told you through the years, in every visit you made to the prison or every letter or email you exchanged. We make lists of places he mentioned, places he talked about visiting again one day, any people still in this area whom he might turn to for help. And we make a plan to lure him into a trap."

A trap for Brian, just like the trap closing in around her. She shivered even though the air-conditioning wasn't all that successful in keeping out the brutal summer heat.

"If I don't help you, my brother could be killed and I go to jail. If I do help you, he could still be killed, but you'll do your best not to kill him. And even then, he faces the possibility of the death penalty. In return, I have no guarantees that I won't go to jail at some point too. Do I have it right? That's the so-called deal you're offering?"

The fight seemed to drain out of him, leaving him looking tired, almost defeated. "That's the deal. I know it's not much. But it's the best I can offer."

"Okay."

His eyes widened. "Okay? Just like that?"

"I'm not an idiot, Colin. I can see for myself that you're right about the danger that Brian's in. And I can't help him while sitting in a jail cell. I'm going to have to trust that the Colin I once knew is still inside you somewhere—the man with honor, integrity and mercy. I'm putting my faith, and my brother's life, in your hands. We have a deal."

Chapter Four

After conferring again with some other officers, Colin returned to the desk. "The police are gathering in the main conference room to ask you some questions," he told her. "They'll let us know when they're ready."

Peyton followed his gaze to a door on the other side of the room. "The police? You make it sound like you aren't one of them."

"I'm not." His eyes hardened like brittle chips of ice. "Guess I neglected to formally introduce myself given our past…association." He pulled an ID badge out of his pants pocket and held it up. "Deputy US Marshal Colin McKenzie. At your service."

She ignored the gibe about their past, and his sarcasm, even though it was hard to keep absorbing his barbs without lashing out. That wouldn't do her or her brother any good. Still, she secretly admitted that the shiny silver circle with a five-point star in the middle that said United States Marshal made her proud. He'd followed his dream, kept his family legacy alive by going into law enforcement like his prosecutor mother and federal judge father. The Mighty McKenzie must be very proud of his third-born son. She wondered if his brothers had pursued similar careers.

"I didn't realize there was a US Marshals office in Gatlinburg."

"There isn't." He slid his badge back into his pocket. "Knoxville's the nearest field office. But that's not where I work most of the time. Usually, I'm on task-forces throughout the state. Last week I started a new assignment here, working out of the Gatlinburg police station as a liaison, tracking down fugitives with outstanding warrants. Cold cases, basically."

That explained why she hadn't seen him around town since she'd gotten back. She'd both hoped for and dreaded bumping into him at some point.

"And you've been assigned to hunt down Brian?"

"No. A team of marshals was assembled out of Memphis to recapture him and the others immediately after the escape. The only reason I'm involved is because when I heard Brian was spotted heading toward this area, I decided to check out your place, just in case he went home. I was surprised to find that he had."

"No more surprised than I was."

His jaw tightened. "Your interference allowed him to get away."

"I'm—"

"Sorry. Yes. I know."

An uncomfortable silence settled between them until an officer opened the conference room door and waved at them.

"That's our cue. Chief Landry is ready to talk to you." Colin motioned for her to precede him. "It's a full house. Given the need to pass along any useful information to the search teams as quickly as possible, the team leads are all in there, as well as detectives. That's why they're in a conference room instead of one of the smaller interview rooms."

She wiped her suddenly sweaty palms against her jeans and headed toward the open door. But ten feet away, he stopped her with a hand on her shoulder.

"Do you know where Brian's hiding?"

"No. I don't. I swear."

He nodded. "All right. We'll talk later, in private, and try to figure out where he might be holed up. But if you do have any ideas and are asked about him in that room, tell the truth. Deal or not. Lying will only get you in more trouble."

"But I don't want Brian hurt. Won't telling them put his life in jeopardy?"

"Tell the truth," he repeated. "The second you feel like you know where he might be, I'll be the first one out the door trying to find him. I'll do everything I can to protect him. You have my word."

"Why? Why do you even want to help him, or me? And don't tell me it's because of my parents."

His brows raised. "You and I may be over, but I loved you once. If nothing else, for the sake of what we once were to each other, I feel obligated to keep you both safe. Is that so difficult to understand?"

"After everything that's happened, yes. It is. You're a far better person than me, Colin. In your place, I don't know that I could be so accommodating."

He frowned and started to say something but the officer who'd waved at them earlier motioned at them again.

Peyton didn't move. "Should I be asking for a lawyer?" she whispered.

He turned his back to the officer. "Probably. Are you asking for one?"

She considered her meager finances and the staggering cost of Brian's continued legal bills that had crippled her entire family financially. It would take her years to pay off her portion of his lawyer fees. Adding more legal costs on top of that would be devastating. "No. I'll just wing it, I guess."

He frowned. "If you can't afford one, I can take care of—"

"No." She cleared her throat and lowered her voice. "No, but thank you for offering. That's very…nice of you, especially considering…" Her voice trailed off. The air between them seemed to thicken with tension. She glanced at the white lines on his hands. How he could have gone through what he had and offer to help her was beyond her comprehension, in spite of his insistence that he felt obligated because of their past.

It felt a thousand ways wrong.

She could never take his money, even though she knew he'd never miss it. Money had never been a concern for any of the McKenzies. They'd become wealthy the old-fashioned way. They'd inherited it. Colin didn't work because he had to. He worked because he wanted to. But that wouldn't make it right for her to take advantage of his generosity.

He studied her, as if deciding whether or not to argue the point. Then he shrugged and led her to the conference room.

It took a supreme effort of will not to turn around

and run when she saw the people waiting for her inside. A dozen men and women went silent at her approach. Each of them had a legal pad or an electronic tablet on the table in front of them. And every one of them was watching her like a scientist observing a particularly nasty insect through a microscope.

"Over there." A lean, middle-aged man with skin the color of an old saddle waved toward two empty chairs directly across the table from him.

She took one of the chairs. Colin took the other.

The man who'd motioned them to sit down gave her a smile that was polite, but far from warm. "I'm Chief Landry. Obviously, you already know Deputy US Marshal McKenzie. Everyone else in this room is either a regular police officer or a detective working for me. Miss Sterling, I want to make it clear that you're not under arrest. I'm going to ask you some questions and, hopefully, you'll do me the courtesy of answering them. You're free to go at any time. Do you understand?"

She glanced longingly at the door but nodded. She understood more than he realized. The legal system wasn't exactly a stranger to her given her family's history fighting the charges against her brother. By not arresting her, the chief didn't have to tell her about her legal rights or remind her that she could have an attorney present. She probably should go ahead and ask for a lawyer, in spite of the cost. But she didn't want to prolong this any more than necessary. She'd just see how things went. Although how they could look worse than they did right now was beyond her.

A stack of folders sat to Landry's right. He took the top one and set it on the table in front of him. He flipped it open, revealing an ugly window into the past, half a dozen color photographs that he methodically lined up in the middle of the table.

The burned-out hull of a building, smoke rising as fire fighters doused the embers.

The dance hall with scores of students clustered in small groups, being questioned by the police.

The ambulance taking Colin away.

Beside her, Colin tensed in his chair.

"Brief history for those in the room unfamiliar with Brian Sterling's case." Landry pulled a sheet of paper from the thick folder and ran a finger across a bulleted list. "The only son of Molly and Benjamin Sterling, Brian was suspected of setting five separate fires as a juvenile but was never convicted, mainly because no one was hurt, the damage was minimal and his parents agreed to make restitution to the property owners as well as take their son to a therapist. That all changed when, at the age of nineteen…" He frowned and flipped the page as if looking for something else. "This doesn't look right. He was a senior in high school? At nineteen?"

Peyton's chest tightened. She hadn't known about the fires. That hadn't come out at the trial. It must have been part of a sealed juvenile record that the chief had convinced some judge to let him access. Her parents, and her brother, had hidden that information from her. Why? To keep her from doubting her brother's innocence? If whatever had happened in his past was relevant in any way to the accusations against him when he was nineteen, the judge at his arson trial would have unsealed the records. Her parents should have trusted her to understand that, and to know that she would continue her support and faith in her brother. She knew him better than anyone. She loved him. Unsealed records thrown at her in a room full of police who wanted to hurt him didn't change that. She drew a shaky breath and forced herself to answer the chief's question.

"Brian had…difficulties in school. He was held back a year, so he was a senior the same time I was even though he's a year older than me."

"Thank you, Miss Sterling. Says here that a few weeks before graduation, Gatlinburg–Pittman High School held a dance at a place called The Barn, a combination restaurant and dance hall on a nature preserve just inside the Great Smoky Mountains National Park. Toward the end of the evening, Brian poured accelerant on the dilapidated original barn that was no longer used for dances, and set it on fire."

"Wrong."

He glanced up at Peyton. "Excuse me?"

"My brother didn't set the fire."

"Twelve jurors disagree with you and sentenced him to fifteen years in prison."

"Juries wrongly convict innocent people all the time. I'm sure you've heard of DNA exonerating people after they've spent years in prison for crimes someone else committed."

He sat back and glanced at Colin before continuing. "I can only deal with the facts as they stand right now. Your brother is a convicted arsonist. There were two people in that barn—"

"No one was supposed to be inside. No Trespassing and Danger signs were posted outside."

"Yes, well, that doesn't change the fact that a pair of randy teenagers snuck away from the chaperones at the dance and hid inside the barn for a make-out session."

Her mother had been one of those chaperones. *Why couldn't you have kept a better eye on them, Mom?*

"When your brother set the fire—" He held up his hands to stop the denial she'd been ready to make. "When the structure went up in flames and the couple was overcome by smoke and trapped by those flames, Deputy US Marshal McKenzie, at the time a senior at the same high school, rescued those people at no small cost to himself, as I'm sure you're aware."

"Yes." She swallowed hard. "I'm well aware."

Colin rested his forearms on the table. "Thank you for that history lesson, chief." His droll tone said that he was anything but thankful. "What you all need to know is that Brian Sterling is a convicted arsonist with a complete disregard for human life."

Peyton stiffened.

"You should consider him armed and dangerous. Approach with extreme caution. And be aware that if cornered, he could resort to setting a fire in order to escape. Now, Chief Landry, I believe you had some questions for Miss Sterling that might assist your teams in narrowing the search area?"

Landry seemed to take Colin's interruption in stride and readily moved on to discuss her brother's escape, along with three other convicts, grilling her with questions as he did so. At one point, he announced that marshals had questioned her father at his Memphis home, immediately after the escape, due to his close proximity to the site. Benjamin Sterling had denied any involvement, not that Peyton would have expected otherwise. Her father had always been one of Brian's harshest critics. It was always she, and her mom, who stood up for him. The fact that the marshals had even considered that her father would help Brian was ludicrous.

"Your father claimed not to know where you were or how to contact you," the chief said. "Do you know why he'd do that? He didn't tell the marshals that you'd moved back to Gatlinburg."

She clutched the edge of her seat beneath the table. "I imagine he thought he was protecting me. Having police at my business or home would have stirred up all the old gossip. It could hurt my café, the life I'm trying to build here." And more important to her father, smear the precious Sterling name once again. Reputation was everything to her dad, far more important than his family.

The chief gave her a skeptical look then studied the notes in front of him. "Says here your mother passed away several months ago."

She could feel Colin's stare beside her. He'd seemed surprised to hear that she owned a café. And at the mention of her mom's death, he seemed genuinely shocked. She regretted that he'd found out this way. But that didn't mean that she was prepared to discuss the details. She was barely holding herself together. Discussing her mom right now would destroy her.

"My mother's death has nothing to do with what's going on with Brian. I'm not going to talk about her."

To her surprise, Landry nodded and moved to other questions. She began to wonder whether talking about her mom would have been easier than hearing the details of her brother's escape. Landry's account of what had happened had nausea coiling in her stomach.

Brian was being transported along with three other convicts to the courthouse in downtown Memphis. Apparently, his lawyer had gotten him a hearing about alleged inhumane conditions at the prison. Since Peyton was well versed in the lawyer's tactics, having worked many an odd job to help her parents pay for all those billable hours, she highly doubted that Brian was being treated unfairly. This latest complaint was likely based on Brian's desire to get some time out of his cell. And he'd apparently taken advantage of the situation by escaping from the prison transport van.

"—and you claim you didn't know anything about your brother's plan?"

She clasped her hands in her lap. "Again, no, Chief Landry. As I've said repeatedly, I didn't even know that he was out of prison until I saw him in my kitchen. Even then, it didn't quite register. I thought his lawyer must have finally managed to get his sentence shortened and Brian wanted to surprise me. Before today, I hadn't seen him in a little over three months."

"Then you didn't know that shortly after he and three other men got away, they were confronted by Memphis police officer Owen Jennings and one of them shot and killed him?"

She drew a shaky breath. "My heart goes out to Officer Jennings and his family. But, no, I didn't know anything about it. I still don't. How did they escape? How did the man who shot Officer Jennings get a gun?"

"You mean how did *your brother* get the gun? Deputy Marshal McKenzie has told me he used to take you and your brother target practicing when you were teen-agers. So we know your brother's more than capable of handling a weapon."

She glanced at Colin, then back at Landry. "Are you saying that you know that Brian is the one who shot Officer Jennings? Not one of the others?"

"No. He's not." Colin sat forward in his chair, his gaze riveted on the police chief. "Dash cam video from the officer's patrol car shows him getting shot and the four prisoners running from the scene. Which man shot him is still to be determined."

The chief sighed. "Marshal McKenzie, you're here as a courtesy due to your close ties to the original arson case, and because you located Mr. Sterling earlier today in an unfortunately failed attempt to apprehend him. I'd appreciate you not interfering in my questioning of Miss Sterling."

"Stick to what's relevant and I won't interfere."

The chief smiled, seeming to shrug off Colin's ad-monition. Peyton figured the two must have a solid friendship, or at least mutual respect, for Landry not to be upset.

"I'm okay moving on to the question of an alibi. Miss Sterling, where were you yesterday morning between the hours of ten and eleven?"

"Alibi? For what?"

"We need to know who might have, and might still be, helping the four convicts who escaped during transport from the Federal Correctional Institution in Memphis yesterday morning. So, again, can you please account for your whereabouts?"

"You seriously think I would have helped them?"

"Peyton." Colin spoke softly beside her. "Just answer the question."

"No," she said. "No, I wasn't six hours away in Memphis while simultaneously at my shop here in Gatlinburg."

"Your shop? I believe you mentioned a café earlier?" Landry asked.

"Yes. I own a café and gift shop combination called Peyton's Place. It's in The Village, off Parkway. It's new, not far from The Hofbrauhaus restaurant."

"Can someone there vouch for where you were yesterday?"

"Joan—she works for me—she can tell you I was there all day, as I am most days. But she's not there right now. The shop closed at six. It will open again in the morning, at nine."

"I'm sure you understand the urgency of verifying your alibi as quickly as possible. Waiting until morning isn't an option. Joan's last name? Her address?"

"Fairmont, Joan Fairmont. I should call her first and let her know that—"

"If you do, that will destroy the credibility of her as an alibi witness. One of my men will head over there now and speak to her. The address?"

She hesitated. "I don't want them frightened by a policeman knocking on their door."

"Them?"

"I have two employees. Joan is full-time, Melissa's part-time. They're roommates."

He motioned to one of the detectives who then wrote something down on the legal pad in front of him. Apparently he was making notes about her alibi.

"And why would they be frightened if a detective knocks on their door? Do they have something to hide?"

Her face heated. "Of course not. But they…they both have criminal records." She could practically feel Colin's gaze burning into her. "Nothing dangerous or anything. They were both homeless and became friends while trying to survive on the streets. They were hungry and got caught shoplifting at a grocery store. Both did a few months in the local jail."

"Are there any other criminals working at your shop that we need to know about?"

She had to count to ten before she could speak without yelling. "I don't consider Joan and Melissa to be *criminals*. Being poor and hungry are hardly crimes. They made restitution for what little food they took when they were practically starving. And they're working hard to turn their lives around."

"No doubt. My apologies if I seemed insensitive."

His sincere tone went a long way toward defusing her anger. She gave him a crisp nod, accepting his apology.

"Any other employees?"

She hesitated.

"Miss Sterling?"

She glanced at Colin, but his stormy eyes gave her no indication of what he was thinking. "Technically, no. But Mr. Hardy comes by to perform odd jobs for food. He… I believe he may have had some scrapes with the law as well."

Colin focused his gaze on a spot on the far wall.

"Do you have Mr. Hardy's address so we can speak to him too?" Landry asked.

"I don't think he has an address. I've offered to let

him sleep in our storage room. But he always declines, says something about the stars being his roof."

"How often does he come around?"

"Pretty much every day. But there's no need to bother him. Joan will corroborate what I told you about being at the shop." She rattled off Joan and Melissa's address at the halfway house where they lived. "Please be polite and nonjudgmental when you speak to them. They've had a hard time of it and have been wonderful friends and workers."

"I'm sure we can figure out how to ask them a few questions without traumatizing or insulting them."

Since she was feeling a bit traumatized herself, she had little faith in his statement. She wrapped her arms around her middle. How much more of this interrogation was she going to have to endure?

The detective who'd been taking notes about Joan and Melissa picked up his legal pad and left the room.

"Last question, Miss Sterling."

Thank God.

"You said you haven't seen your brother in three months, prior to him showing up in your home yesterday. Do you have any ideas about where he might hide given that we've got roadblocks and checkpoints all throughout the county?"

She shook her head. "No. I honestly don't. It's not like he has any friends left around here. Our house is the only place I'd expect him to go."

"If you think of something, you'll let me know?"

"Of course." Would she? She had no idea. If Brian had indeed killed a police officer, she'd be the first one to turn him in. But he'd been falsely convicted of one crime already. Trusting the police and the judicial system not to pin something else on him wasn't likely to happen. And she really hadn't had time to consider where he might hide. Where *would* he go if he was hunkering down, trying to keep someone from finding him?

The chief motioned to one of the detectives a few seats down, who then got up and handed him the tablet he'd been using during the meeting. Landry studied it a few moments, then turned it around and slid it across the table to Peyton. "Officer Redding typed up your statement, everything you said during our chat."

Chat? If this was a chat, she couldn't imagine how awful a real interrogation would have been.

He tapped the screen, scrolling to the top of the form. "Read through that. If you agree that it's accurate, sign at the bottom. If anything needs correction, have Marshal McKenzie get Detective Redding back in here. Make yourself comfortable while we confirm your alibi. You don't have your phone do you? I don't want you calling your employees."

She automatically felt her jeans pockets. "No. Actually, I don't. I think it's in my purse. But I'm not even sure where I left my purse." A feeling of panic settled in her stomach as she tried to remember where it might be. Her credit cards and pretty much her entire life was in there.

"It's locked in my desk," Colin said. "I think your phone was in the side pocket."

She smiled in relief. "Thank you."

He nodded.

"That's settled then." Landry shoved his chair back

and stood. The other people in the room began filing out the door.

"Chief Landry?" she asked.

He paused. "Yes?"

"You seem to be focused entirely on my brother in regards to the escape and the death of Officer Jennings. Is there a reason for that? There were three other convicts involved, based on what you said earlier."

He smiled. "I assure you that we're looking into all four men and speaking to anyone who knows them. Perhaps I should have asked just to be sure—have you ever met Damon Patterson, Vincent Snyder or Tyler King?"

"None of those names sound familiar, no. Are they the convicts from the van? Do you think they're still with my brother or did they split up?"

He smiled. "Thank you again for your cooperation." He left the room, closing the door behind him.

Peyton clutched the tablet in front of her, painfully aware that the chief hadn't answered her questions. "What happens next?" she asked, without looking at Colin beside her.

"We wait. And hope that your alibi checks out."

"It will. I wasn't in Memphis yesterday. You believe me, right?" This time she turned to look at him.

He stared at her a long moment, then stood and crossed to the door.

"Colin? You do believe me, don't you?"

"I'm getting a bottle of water. Want anything?"

She slowly shook her head and he left the room.

Chapter Five

It was bad enough that crime scene investigators were combing through every inch of Peyton's family home, having obtained a search warrant based on Brian being inside earlier today. What was even more humiliating was standing in her own bedroom while a police woman rifled through the bag that Peyton had just packed.

Peyton crossed her arms, frowning at the woman's profile as she wadded up shirts and pants that Peyton had painstakingly rolled to avoid wrinkles. The woman pulled out yet another pair of Peyton's underwear, letting the red thong dangle in the air. What did she think? That Peyton was going to smuggle a gun in her undies and attack Colin in his sleep?

"I don't think they're your size," she snapped, unable to put up with the farce any longer.

Unruffled, the officer smiled politely, underwear still suspended in the air. "I'm just doing my job, Miss Sterling."

"Is there a problem in here?" Colin stepped into the room.

Peyton snatched the thong and tossed it into the overnight bag. "Not at all. Officer…"

"Simmons," the policewoman supplied, sounding infuriatingly amused.

"Right. Officer Simmons was just complimenting me on my fabric choices. Isn't that right?"

Simmons rolled her eyes. "You have a nice evening, ma'am." She stepped past Peyton, nodding at Colin before exiting the room.

"Did I miss something?" Colin asked.

She straightened the contents of the bag as best she could without dumping everything out and starting over. "I'm fairly certain that Officer Simmons was wrinkling my clothes and going as slowly as humanly possible just because—"

"Because you knocked a gun out of a marshal's hand and let a suspected cop killer get away?"

She stood frozen, his words sinking in. Shame made her face heat. "You're right. I'm so used to being on the defensive about Brian being innocent that I didn't look at it from her perspective."

He stepped to the bed and zipped her bag closed, then hefted it in his hand. "Maybe she was suspicious because you've packed half your bedroom in here. I bet this would require extra baggage fees at the airport."

"It's not *that* heavy. I know I packed more than I need for one night. But I always worry that I'll want something else after I've left the house."

"It's a good thing you did. I don't expect you'll be able to come back here for several days." He motioned toward the doorway. "Let's go."

"I can carry my own…wait. What do you mean *several days*? I have to do laundry, clean the house, work on the store's books, and a hundred other things. I can't put my life on hold."

"Why not? Think of it as a vacation. Don't worry about anything except helping me figure out where your brother might be hiding."

"I don't know what you were expecting but I can't ignore my responsibilities. I have to be back at the store Sunday and Monday. Those are Joan's days off. Melissa can't run the store by herself. This is the busy summer tourist season. Besides, my customers expect fresh baked goods Sunday through Friday. If I don't have new product in the display cases, I lose business. I'm still operating in the red, struggling to make this work as it is."

"If money's your worry, I can—"

"No. We've already had that conversation. I appreciate your generous offer, truly. But come early Sunday morning, I need to be in my own kitchen baking. Then I'm going to the shop."

He set the bag back on the bed. "Unless your brother and the other escapees are either caught or known to be in an area far from here by Sunday, you're not coming back. And you definitely aren't going into town."

"Colin—"

"Your brother showed up here once already. Odds are, he'll try again. The reports my fellow marshals have been sharing with me indicate that all four men were spotted traveling together at their last verified sighting. One of them is a convicted murderer with ties to gangs. Until I know it's safe, you aren't coming back here. Period."

Her throat went dry. Her brother was traveling with a

convicted murderer? Brian wasn't exactly street-smart. Even after years in prison, he still seemed like a scared, naive kid every time she visited him.

Please be careful. Don't get yourself killed, Brian.

Since Colin was watching her, she forced a smile. "When you put it that way, I understand your concerns. I'll need to check whether Joan and Melissa can take on additional shifts for a few days." Not that she could afford the extra pay. And she didn't know if her employees could change their schedules last minute. "Since my alibi was verified, it's okay to call them, right?"

"Of course. Tomorrow."

"Right." The dark glass of her bedroom window clearly showed it was too late to call anyone tonight. "I'll need to grab my baking supplies and take them to your place so I can bake things for the shop. I can ask Joan to come pick them up. Is that okay? Me using your kitchen?"

"You're welcome to use my kitchen. But let's head over there first and see if I already have what you need instead of hauling half your things over there."

"Why can't we just grab my stuff while we're still here?"

He blew out a breath. "Because the crime scene unit is still collecting evidence. Allowing you to take clothes and toiletries is one thing. Hauling out pots and pans and who knows what else is completely different." He motioned her toward the hallway and hefted her bag again.

The warrant. It all came down to that. She shook her head and headed down the hallway, Colin's boots echoing against the hardwood behind her. Just inside the family room, she had to stop to let a tech pass by with a laptop in a clear plastic bag.

"Hey, wait. That's mine. My business records are on that computer. I'll need that to work on invoices tomorrow." She reached for the bag. Colin pulled her against his side, nodding at the other man to continue out the propped-open front door.

"What are you doing?" She shook his arm off her shoulders.

"Keeping you from getting arrested for interfering with the execution of a search warrant. Come on. We need to get out of here."

She mumbled beneath her breath just what she thought of the search warrant but dutifully started toward the front door. When she saw Officer Simmons lounging on her couch like a plant taking root, she stopped again. "Shouldn't you be rifling through my underwear drawer or something?"

Simmons's eyes widened.

Colin coughed, then cleared his throat. "Sorry," he told Simmons.

"What are you apologizing to her for? Why is she—"

He took a firm grip on her arm and steered her out of the house, not slowing down until they were standing beside the open passenger door of his ridiculously tall pickup. White vans surrounded them, several parked right on the pitiful patch of weeds and dirt that used to be her mama's front lawn.

She gasped when another tech passed her carrying a precious family photo album. "Hey! Give that back. What are you doing with—oh!"

Colin lifted her up and deposited her onto the passenger seat and then reached for the seat belt as if she was a toddler. She snatched it from him and clicked it into place.

"I can fasten my own seat belt. And I could have climbed up into this monster truck of yours without help."

"No. You couldn't. You're so short you could pass for a hobbit."

She gasped in outrage.

He shut the door with more force than was necessary.

She crossed her arms, jaw clenched as she watched the vultures hauling out more of her things. A few seconds later, Colin hopped up on the driver's seat without a bit of trouble, making her resent him for his long legs. He tossed her bag onto the bench seat between them and sat there, as if waiting for something.

She clenched her jaw tighter, determined not to say another word.

Thunder rumbled overhead. In the distance, a flash of lightning lit up the sky for a few brief seconds. Yet another summer storm was moving into the area.

"I hope the rain turns the road into a river and those stupid vans slide into a ditch," she grumbled.

"There it is." He sounded almost cheerful as he started the engine. "*Now* we can go."

She crossed her arms. "You think you know me so well."

The almost smile that had accompanied his announcement faded and once again the sullen stranger took his place. "No. I don't think I know you at all. Not anymore, if I ever did."

His words were like a punch in the gut, reminding

her of just how much water had passed beneath the bridge since they'd last been together.

He backed out of the driveway, the wheels kicking up gravel when he headed up the road.

Up.

Not down.

Unfamiliar terrain passed by her window, what little she could see in the moonlight. When she'd lived here before, this road had dead-ended just past her house. She hadn't realized since coming back that it continued around the mountain.

"Is this a shortcut?" she asked.

"No." He rounded a curve, the grade getting steeper as they continued higher.

"Colin, where…" White wood fencing appeared off to their left, illuminated by spotlights and marching across the fields as far as she could see. Another curve revealed even more landscape lights, on either side of a long, paved driveway. And at the end sat a huge white two-story farmhouse with an enormous wraparound porch, complete with a porch swing. She smiled sadly at the swing. She'd always wanted one but never had one growing up. Her dad had said their porch was too small.

"Beautiful house. Adore the swing," she said, more to herself than to him. "Is this where we're going?"

He nodded.

"Who lives there? Another police officer? You're going to have someone else ask me questions about Brian?"

He shook his head and turned up the drive. When they reached the garage, he pressed a button in the roof of his truck and the door began to rise.

"This is *your* house?"

"I built it a handful of years ago."

He pulled into the three-car garage. An expensive-looking black sports car of some type was parked two spaces away.

"I thought you had a chalet on Skyline Drive?"

He shot her a surprised glance. "I used to. How did you know about the chalet? I bought it a year after you left." He cut the engine.

She shrugged, unwilling to admit that she'd ruthlessly grilled an old friend for information about Colin after being forced to move to Memphis. "One of dad's clients or mom's old church friends probably mentioned it on the phone after we first left. But I never knew you built a new home a few miles up the road from mine. Why did you? Why here?"

He hesitated. "The land was available, the area familiar. No neighbors to worry about."

"And you just happened to build a white two-story farmhouse surrounded by acres of white fencing? With a porch swing? Like we talked about building together one day?"

His hands gripped the steering wheel so hard that his knuckles turned white. "I've always liked this style of home. Don't read anything into it."

She jerked back, and hated that she had. He'd hurt her, again, and she seemed helpless to hide it every time one of his barbs hit the bullseye.

His expression softened with regret. "Peyton—"

"I'll get the door myself this time." She grabbed her purse and overnight bag and hopped out of the truck before he could get out and help her. She stumbled but considered it a victory that she didn't do a face-plant on the pristine gray-painted floor of the garage. In comparison, her garage had cracks and oil stains all over the place from her constantly leaking SUV. She'd be afraid to park her car in something this clean.

Both of them were silent as he led the way into the house.

Similar to her home, the garage led into a laundry/mudroom. But that was where the similarities ended. They walked down a wide back hall with several doors, all closed. A cased opening led them toward the front of the house, around a concrete-and-metal staircase into a massive vaulted family room. They finally stopped in the kitchen in the back-left corner of the house.

Her mouth dropped open. She nearly drooled. What she'd considered to be a high-end redesign of her own kitchen seemed like a joke compared to Colin's. It was completely open to the main room with a massive island the only separation. Four saddle-style bar stools covered in black leather with matching black iron legs were snugged up beneath the overhang of the island on the side facing the family room. There wasn't a table and chairs anywhere that she saw. And she hadn't seen a dining room on their quick trip through the house. She wondered if he ate all his meals at the island or off trays in front of the television like she tended to do.

The ceilings soared up two stories high with skylights that allowed a breathtaking view of the stars. During the day, it would be awash with sunlight. Just like they'd imagined when they'd talked about their future together and the house where they one day hoped to live.

He opened a door and flipped on the light switch.

"I wanted to show you the pantry since you were worried about baking supplies. My mom insists on keeping it stocked for when she comes over for family gatherings. She enjoys baking too, like you and your mom. I imagine most of what you need is in here."

She ducked inside the enormous walk-in that was larger than her bedroom back home. Flour, sugar, spices of every kind lined one side, a much better variety than she had in her own pantry. It was a baker's dream. Even if her business started booming, she could never afford something like this. She stepped back, feeling like the poor relation. Which was odd, considering that the McKenzie wealth had never bothered her in the past. Now it seemed like a looming barrier between them.

"Nice. *Really* nice. I'll be sure to reimburse you for any ingredients I use."

"That's not necessa—"

"I'll pay you back or I can't do my baking here. And I really need to have product ready Sunday morning."

His jaw tightened but he didn't argue. "Are you hungry? And don't tell me you won't eat my groceries. You're my guest. I insist."

Guest. What a sad, lonely word. At eighteen, she and Colin had been ready to take on the world together. She'd expected that by twenty-eight she'd be working alongside him, fighting for justice. Coming home every night to a couple of kids, preferably boys with their father's deep blue eyes and blue-black hair. Every night, she'd fall into his arms in the king-size bed and make love until dawn.

"Thanks." Her voice came out barely a whisper. She cleared her throat and tried again. "I couldn't eat anything right now. Actually, I'm kind of exhausted. It's been a rough day all around."

He studied her a moment, as if he wanted to say something. But then he turned and led her back into the family room. He didn't stop until they reached the stairs on the far right side. "The guest bedrooms are upstairs. Pick whichever one you like."

She admired the industrial black metal handrail, smoothed her fingers over the iron cables. Modern farmhouse. A little more masculine and contemporary than she'd have wanted. But gorgeous, just the same. Seeing their dream brought to life—without her— somehow hurt worse than if their dream had never been realized.

"It's beautiful, Colin. Your home is...perfect." She smiled wistfully. "I don't suppose you have a horse barn out back with a palomino mare?"

He shook his head, a faraway look in his eyes. Was he remembering all the times they'd ridden trail ponies through the foothills? Or taken turns on the palomino her father got her for her sixteenth birthday? The same horse she'd had to sell when Brian was arrested and they scraped for every penny to pay for his defense.

"I've got a workshop out back, that's it. You were the one crazy about horses when we were young. Not me."

Her hand tightened on the railing. "I see." She took a deep breath, then another, struggling against the urge to cry. She'd rather die than let loose with another on-slaught of tears in front of him when he was being so cold.

"Make yourself at home." His voice sounded strained. "I'm going to bed." He opened a door to the right of the stairs, a few feet from the main entrance to the house.

He needn't have bothered shutting the door behind him. He'd already shut her out just fine without one.

Chapter Six

Colin slowly lowered himself to his bed and dropped his head into his hands. Bringing Peyton here had seemed like a good idea when he'd originally thought of it. He'd been intent on getting the truth out of her, figuring if they were holed up together he'd wear her down, get her to tell him where her brother was hiding.

At the same time, he had a security system, something he'd noticed she didn't have at her house. She was safer here, especially if her brother had rejoined the other escaped convicts. But until he'd seen the truth dawn in her eyes when she realized he'd built their dream house—without her—he hadn't recognized the real reason that he'd brought her here.

Revenge.

The truth sickened him. He'd hurt her today, over and over. And all it had done was make him disgusted with himself. Not that he'd originally set out to build this house hoping to rub her face in it. His motivations had been even more pathetic. He'd loved her so much that he'd convinced himself that if he built their dream house, he'd be able to bridge the gap between them. He would talk her into coming back to Gatlinburg to recapture what they'd once had. But, of course, that hadn't happened.

He'd gone to Memphis, the day after the house was finished, and knocked on her father's door asking to see her. Mr. Sterling had shaken his head and told him he was too late, that Peyton had gotten married. Colin had gone to a hotel and dived into a case of whiskey. He'd probably still be there if his brothers hadn't tracked him down and forced him to go home and sober up.

A few months later, he'd gone back, determined to man up, congratulate her on her marriage and wish her a happy life. But he hadn't even known her new last name. And when he'd turned onto the street where her father lived, he couldn't work up the nerve to get out of his truck and ask about Peyton.

Once again, he'd hit the whiskey. Once again, his interfering brothers wouldn't let him wallow in self-pity. Slowly, painstakingly, he'd pulled himself out of the gutter and figured out how to build a reasonably contented life without her. And he had, eventually. Or so he'd thought. Until he'd stepped into her kitchen today and she'd chosen her brother over him. Again.

Just like that day at the barn, when the police had Brian in their squad car and Colin was in the back of an ambulance. She could either have gone with Brian to the station or with Colin to the hospital. She'd chosen Brian. And other than at the trial, surrounded by a room full of other people, Colin had never seen her again until today. She'd opened all the old wounds by choosing an arsonist, a cop killer, over the man she'd once planned to spend the rest of her life with.

All the old resentments and memories had bubbled

to the surface, leaving him stewing in frustration and anger and pain. He'd selfishly wanted her to feel the same pain. So he'd made that stupid deal with her to get her out here.

After seeing her eyes widen when his house appeared over the hill, hearing the joy in her voice when she'd mentioned the porch swing that Colin knew she'd always wanted, he'd realized what a horrible jerk he was being. He never should have built the house. And he certainly never should have brought Peyton here.

That wasn't all he'd realized tonight.

He'd realized something far worse—that she still had the power to set his blood on fire. In spite of all the years, all the progress he'd thought he'd made, he still cared about her. And he wanted her, oh how he wanted her. He wanted her naked skin heating his, her silky hair fanned across his pillow. He wanted his name on her lips when she climaxed beneath him. He shuddered and squeezed his hands into fists, drawing deep breaths.

Not that it helped.

Thunder rumbled overhead. He stood, crossed to the front bedroom window and looked down the road, at the line of trees at the end of the driveway. Lightning flashed. Wind and rain whipped the trees as if they were no more substantial than blades of grass. But the storm outside was nothing compared to the storm raging inside him.

He was a coward. Running in here had been a spineless act of desperation. He'd wanted to escape, put some distance between himself and Peyton before he did something even more foolish than he'd already done.

Like kiss her.

If Peyton was still downstairs, if she hadn't gone up to bed yet, he should go back out there and beg her forgiveness. He should take her somewhere else. She shouldn't have to stay in this house with him, where everywhere she looked was a reminder of the plans they'd once made together.

He cursed and stalked to the door. But when he put his hand on the doorknob, he couldn't bring himself to turn it. He needed one more minute, maybe ten, to stop the flood of images that seeing her again had unleashed.

What he really needed was a bottle of whiskey.

He squeezed his eyes shut and rested his forehead against the door. But closing his eyes did nothing to block out the memories.

Peyton's sixteenth birthday, her silver-gray eyes alight with excitement as she sat atop the palomino mare that she'd been begging her parents to buy for months.

Peyton smiling at Colin while wearing a figure-hugging black sequined dress that had him choking on his own tongue.

Peyton, a few weeks before graduation, lying on a blanket covered in nothing but her strawberry blond hair—and Colin—letting him warm her after they'd skinny-dipped beneath a waterfall.

Peyton, Peyton, Peyton. Nearly every treasured memory from his past began and ended with her.

Until one horrible night had ripped them apart.

The barn had burned long ago. But the scars on his arms, and in his heart, throbbed anew as if it had happened yesterday. He curled his fingers against the door and wondered what in the world he was going to do.

Chapter Seven

Thunder boomed outside, storm clouds darkening the sky as if it was still the middle of the night instead of morning. Colin had taken a shower, in spite of all the times his mother had warned him that it was too dangerous during a thunderstorm. But if he followed her advice, it would be the middle of next week before he got clean again. This storm showed no signs of letting up.

As he buttoned his shirt, it dawned on him that the low rumble he was hearing now wasn't thunder. He moved to his front bedroom window and saw a white Jeep barreling up the road, windshield wipers making little progress against the sheets of rain whipping against the glass.

Green stripes and a National Park Service emblem on the door told him it was probably one of his brothers. He groaned in frustration as more lightning cracked overhead. Hopefully Peyton was still asleep. He didn't want his family to know she was here. That would open up a whole new round of intrusion into his life that he didn't want to deal with right now. They'd probably start an intervention and take all the whiskey again.

A knock sounded on the bedroom door. "Colin?"

So much for Peyton being asleep.

The knock sounded again. "Someone's coming up the—"

He opened the door. "Morning, Peyton." She was sexy as hell in a white tank top and matching capris that bared too much smooth, golden skin for his comfort. His mouth went dry as he tried not to let his traitorous gaze dip to that tempting valley between her breasts.

She backed up a step, smoothing her hands on her pants in the nervous gesture he remembered so well. "Good morning. Sorry to bother you. I just wanted to make sure you know that you're about to have company. It looks like some kind of official vehicle from the Park Service. Do you think…" She cleared her throat. "Do you think someone found Brian already?"

Thunder rumbled overhead.

"Not likely. The search in this area was halted last night because of the storm. They won't be able to risk going out again until the lightning stops. Which probably won't be any time soon."

A horn honked out front.

He motioned toward the back hallway. "Do you mind? I need to open the garage—"

"Oh, sorry." She moved out of his way.

He strode past the stairs and called over his shoulder. "Whoever it is, I'll try to get rid of them. It's ridiculously early for a visit."

"It's nine o'clock. How late do you normally sleep?"

He checked his watch. She was right. It was so dark outside that he hadn't awakened with the sun coming through the windows like he usually did. "Back in a few." He turned down the hall.

The horn honked again. He jogged the rest of the way to the garage. After disabling the alarm, he pressed the button on the wall and waited to see which brother he was about to battle.

When the door cleared the windshield, he groaned. Duncan. His second-oldest brother was even more stubborn than Colin. If he even suspected that Peyton might be here, Duncan wouldn't leave short of a physical threat. Maybe he should go back inside and grab his Glock.

As soon as the Jeep pulled into the middle spot between Colin's truck and car, his brother cut the engine and hopped out, a look of concern on his face.

"I heard our resident arsonist graduated to cop-killer and is back in town. You need my help catching the bastard?"

"Good morning to you too. And, no. Thanks, but half the state is looking for him already. There's no need for you to take off work to help. Speaking of work..." He glanced at his watch and winced. "I'm running really late today. You should probably head back out. I need to get out of here."

Duncan narrowed his eyes. "It's Saturday."

"I work Saturdays. Sometimes."

"Since when?"

"Since whenever I need to." He motioned toward Duncan's Jeep. "Do you mind? Your little Special Agent car is dripping all over my garage."

Duncan rolled his eyes and stopped in front of Colin. He looked him up and down, skepticism heavy in his expression. "You Deputy US Marshal guys are getting sloppy these days. You normally wear jeans to work?"

"On Saturdays."

"Right. Where's your vest? And gun?"

Colin made a show of surprise, patting his shirt and then looking down at his hip. "Son of a…well, I'll have to grab those. Too much going on these days. I'm not thinking clearly."

"Like what? What *exactly* is going on?"

"Felons on the loose, like you said. Kind of my specialty so I need to get on it." He motioned toward the Jeep. "If you don't mind backing out—"

"Because you're on your way to work."

"Yep."

"On a Saturday."

"Mm-hmm."

"At nine in the morning, in jeans, without your Kevlar or sidearm. Yeah, I'm not buying that. Try for something more believable."

Colin crossed his arms. "Do you always have to be so difficult?"

"Remi says I'm charming."

"Remi's blinded by love. She'll find out the truth after you get married. Poor girl."

"Speaking of the truth—"

Colin lifted his hands in exasperation. "Okay, fine. I overslept and didn't want you ribbing me about it. I'm on my way to the office to look over some notes in my files so I can make a game plan. I figured I could dress down since not many people will be there."

"Whatever you say. What about the other guys who escaped? Have any of them been caught?"

Colin settled back against the wall, crossing his arms again. "Not so far. Have you been getting alerts?"

"Nothing useful. We were told the day of the escape that all four were seen a few hours west of here. Since then we heard someone had sighted Brian close by, but no details. We've got extra patrols out, when we can with this storm. The park's closed, of course. Adam's been running the evacuation. He got the last of the campers out a few hours before the storm hit. Have you heard anything specific about Brian?"

"Not since I saw him yesterday morning." Colin winced.

Duncan pounced on his mistake. "I *knew* it. I figured that little twerp would come after you. Where'd you see him? What happened?"

"Don't you have somewhere else to be?"

"My boss is flexible. I've got nothing but time. Tell me what happened."

Colin shook his head. "Nothing much to tell. After I heard about the escape, I figured I'd check the old Sterling homestead, just in case Brian headed back somewhere familiar. I didn't really expect him to be there. We both pretty much surprised each other and he ended up giving me the slip."

"That sucks. So, you're working the case?"

"Officially, the conflict of interest because Brian set the fire that injured me makes me ineligible."

"So, you're working the case."

"Of course. I took some vacation time. It's not exactly a secret as to why. Chief Landry and the marshal in charge of finding the escapees are both being accommodating. They're willing to share information with me about the status of the search as long as I answer their questions about Brian's personality and history."

"If he's still in the area, there's nowhere he can go. Every main road I've been on this morning has a road block set up, even with the storm. No one's taking any chances. His only choice will be to head into the mountains, hunker down and hope he can outwait law enforcement. From what I remember, he was never the outdoorsy type. I can't imagine him lasting long without breaking into someone's cabin for supplies. That'll make it easy to track him down." He arched a brow. "Unless the guys he's with are better at living off the land and were smart enough to take supplies with them."

"Doubtful, according to the files I read. They're all city slickers."

"I wonder why they came this way."

Colin shrugged as if he had no clue. But he was pretty sure that he knew why. Peyton. In spite of being a year older than his sister, Brian had always relied on her to protect him. Either he'd intended to ask her for help, or she'd known he was coming and was waiting for him already when Colin interfered with their plans.

Lightning cracked outside, creating a strobe-like effect through the garage.

Duncan glanced toward the windows. "Don't get me wrong. This is a nice garage and all. But are you ever gonna ask me inside? The weather's nasty out there."

"You national parks guys can handle it. Although, that road out front does turn into a river sometimes. You really ought to head back down the mountain before it gets any worse."

"I've got a four-wheel drive that sticks to the road like a mountain goat. You aren't worried about me sliding into a ditch. Cut the crap and tell me why you're really trying to get rid of me."

"I think he doesn't want you to know about me."

Colin sighed and turned around. Peyton stood in the doorway, her curly blond hair tousled around her shoulders. Silvery eyes laced with pain pinned him with an accusing stare before she turned around and disappeared into the house.

Duncan's mouth fell open. "Was that who I think it was?"

"Would you believe me if I said no?"

"She's seen the farmhouse, the porch swing?"

"Since she's *in* the farmhouse, I'm guessing that's a yes."

Duncan put his hand on Colin's shoulder. "Where's your whiskey? I need to pour it all out."

"Not. Funny." Colin shoved his brother's arm off his shoulder.

Duncan pulled out his cell phone.

"What are you doing?"

"Calling for reinforcements. Ian, as usual, is incommunicado. What's it been, six months since we saw our prodigal baby brother?" He shrugged. "Adam, however, now there's the typical first-born reliable brother if ever I saw one. He'll drop everything to head over. Maybe I should ask him to bring Mom and Dad too. I bet they'd love to catch up on whatever the hell is going on here."

Colin yanked the phone out of his hand. "Fine. You can come in. But try to behave for once. Keep it professional."

Duncan pressed a hand to his chest. "You wound me,

brother. I always behave." He grinned and strode past Colin into the house.

Colin swore and hurried after him.

Chapter Eight

Eavesdropping on Colin and Duncan's conversation in the garage wasn't Peyton's proudest moment. But no one was telling her anything and she was desperate for news about her brother. All she'd learned was that Colin was so ashamed to be seen with her that he was willing to lie to his own brother.

She was in the kitchen setting up the coffee maker when she heard them come in. She could feel them watching her but she focused on getting things ready instead of turning around. After starting the coffee brewing, she opened the cabinet above it to search for mugs. No searching required. They were right there, above the coffee maker where she kept them in her own kitchen. It made sense. Apparently, Colin thought so too.

The sound of whispering had her tensing. She imagined that Colin was bringing Duncan up to speed about what had happened over the past twenty-four hours. And why he'd dared to bring the dreaded ex into his home.

She grabbed some milk out of the refrigerator and added it to one of the cups—the one for Duncan. She put sugar in hers and left Colin's black. Enough coffee was already in the carafe for her to pour some, so she filled the three mugs before setting the carafe back into place. She drew a bracing breath, then turned around and set the mugs on the white quartz island. Both men stood on the other side, silent now, watching her.

She slid a cup toward each of them, then cradled her own between her hands. "I'm assuming you both take your coffee the same way you did when we were in high school." She blew on hers to cool it, then took a sip.

Duncan shot a look at Colin. They both stepped forward and took their cups.

"Thanks," Duncan said. "Smells great."

Colin took a sip. The corner of his mouth lifted. He nodded his approval and she hated that her stomach jumped with pleasure.

Duncan's smile after taking a sip of his own coffee was kind and generous, but didn't make her stomach flip like Colin's had.

"Perfect for a rainy morning. Thanks, Peyton," Duncan said.

"Is anyone hungry? I haven't had a chance to prepare dough and let it rise. But if Colin has any canned biscuits in the fridge, I can add my special touches and bake us some croissants that will taste great."

"Croissants?" Duncan looked like he was ready to drool. "Like your mom used to make?"

Colin glanced sharply at her, reminding her that she still hadn't discussed with him what had happened to her mom. That was a conversation she hoped to avoid as long as possible.

She smiled, working hard to keep the grief from her expression. "Almost. Like I said, I don't have my spe-

cial recipe dough ready. But I can get it pretty close."
She finally met Colin's probing gaze again. "Do you
have bacon and eggs? Cheese?"

He slowly nodded, concern apparent in his gaze as
he studied her, as if he was worried that she might fall
apart at any moment. But, thankfully, he didn't press
for more information. Not yet anyway.

"Then let's get this party started," she said. "We'll
have bacon, egg and cheese croissants. I'll make enough
croissants so that you can also have some with butter
and honey if you want."

"You don't need to cook for us," Colin said.

"I *want* to cook for us. It won't take long." And baking was a great way to avoid things she didn't want to
talk about.

His sigh could have felled a tree. "Fine. Then we'll
help. Duncan, make yourself useful. Get whatever ingredients she needs from the pantry. I'll get the cookie
sheets and mixer."

She turned around in surprise, a wooden spoon in
her hand. "You want to help?"

"I insist on it." Colin pulled two stainless-steel
cookie sheets from the bottom drawer in the island.

"What do you need from the pantry?" Duncan asked.

She rattled off ingredients and he rushed off to get
them.

Colin opened another drawer in the island, pulled
a full, white apron out and held it up. "Turn around."

She blinked, then turned, holding her hair up as he
lifted the ties around her neck. She hoped he didn't notice the shiver of pleasure when his warm hands touched

her skin. "I'm surprised you'd have any aprons around here."

He finished tying the strings and moved his hands to her waist, pulling those strings back behind her. He was far too close for her peace of mind.

His deep voice rumbled next to her ear when he answered. "I keep them here for my mom."

Mom. There was that word again. She had to breathe through the urge to cry. Thankfully, she had her emotions under control when he finished tying the apron and she turned around.

"Thank you."

"My pleasure."

She stared up into his eyes, admiring how his blue-green shirt deepened the color. And she wished, for just a moment, that she could feel his strong arms wrap around her and pull her in for a hug. She could really use a hug right now, especially from Colin.

"Here you go." Duncan strode in from the pantry, his arms full.

Peyton cleared her throat and stepped back. Then she directed Duncan to set everything down while she got what she needed from the refrigerator.

Colin moved to the island. "Tell us what you want us to do."

Both men looked at her expectantly. The idea of cooking with them was bittersweet and brought back so many good memories from when they were growing up and spending more time at each other's houses than their own. Until that summer when Colin's voice had deepened and her body gained curves she'd never had before, the summer when she and Colin began to look at each other differently and everything changed.

"Okay. Well, do you have a rolling pin?"

Both men started opening drawers in the island on a quest to find one.

By the time they'd finished cooking, eating and restoring the kitchen to its former glory, Peyton had laughed so much her stomach hurt. Duncan's sense of humor was contagious. His fake British accent was awful. His Irish one was much better, which made sense in theory since he was a McKenzie. But she knew none of the brothers had ever been to Ireland. Or, at least, they hadn't before she'd left.

Colin had grinned and laughed right along with his brother, although he was more inclined to elbow him in the ribs or purposely spoil the punchline of one of Duncan's jokes. That was one of the things that Peyton had always loved about the McKenzie brothers—the strong bond between them and how much fun they could have together. Her own brother was quiet and moody, almost fragile. She loved him dearly but could never imagine him horsing around like the McKenzies.

Duncan wiped his hands on a paper towel and tossed it into the trash. "We've talked about my fiancée, our family, Adam's job as a law-enforcement ranger and his new bride. But you haven't told us anything about you. How's your family?" His eyes widened. "I mean, aside from your brother of course."

She glanced at Colin, seeing the unasked questions brimming in his eyes. "Shouldn't we start brainstorming how to find Brian before some trigger-happy searcher gets to him first?"

He exchanged a surprised look with Duncan, she assumed over her less than subtle attempt at changing the subject.

"Sure. We can start right now. I'll get my tablet and we can sit in the family room."

"I think that's my cue to hit the road," Duncan said.

Colin shook his head. "That cue came a long time ago but you chose to ignore it."

Duncan grinned and the brothers pounded each other on the back. He stepped to Peyton and offered her his arm with a wink. "Walk me to my Jeep, pretty lady?"

"What are you doing?" Colin asked, sounding wary.

"Saying goodbye to an old friend. Come on, Peyton. Don't let that ornery bear ruin our fun." He pulled her hand through his arm and tugged her into the family room.

She smiled at Colin and shrugged helplessly. He'd crossed his arms and was watching them intently.

Duncan didn't slow down until they were standing by his SUV. He surprised her again by giving her a quick hug. "It was good seeing you again, sweet colleen, even if the circumstances aren't exactly the best."

"You too. Thanks for being so nice to me. It was… unexpected."

He smiled and turned her hands in his, looking down. "I don't see a wedding ring. You're single?"

She tugged her hands free. "Yes, not that it matters. You're already taken," she teased. "Congratulations on your engagement."

He grinned. "Remi would love you. I think you'll find that everyone in my family still loves you, no matter what."

She blinked, not sure what to say to that.

His gaze flicked toward the door to the mudroom, then back to her. "I can't pretend to understand the choices you made ten years ago. I tell myself that you don't have any idea what all he went through, how much he needed you, or you'd have been there for him."

"Duncan—"

"You hurt him, more than you'll ever know. But I'll tell you something else. I can't remember the last time he laughed and smiled like he did this morning." He pressed his hand to his chest. "Granted, I'm a charming fellow. But it wasn't because of me that he was smiling." He sobered and took her hands in his again. "There's something special there, between you two, always has been. I, for one, am hopeful that it works out this time. He deserves some happiness in his life."

She stared at him in shock. "You've misunderstood why I'm here. It's all about helping Brian, trying to save his life. That's it."

He slowly shook his head. "Dear, sweet lass, my brother's a great guy. But if you think he'd help anyone else in your situation, try to save the man he holds responsible for everything he lost, you're fooling yourself." He kissed her on the cheek, then got into his Jeep.

Peyton wrapped her arms around her waist as he turned the car around on the back-up pad out front, then ventured into the heart of the storm. She didn't know what to think of his little speech. What had he meant when he said that she didn't understand what Colin had gone through, or how much he'd needed her?

Had everything her father told her been a lie?

The garage door started to close. She turned to see Colin leaning against the doorframe behind her.

"Everything okay out here?"

No. She wanted to run to him, throw her arms around him. Tell him how deeply she loved him, that she'd never stopped. The only thing holding her back was that she wasn't sure what he'd do, whether he'd welcome her embrace, or turn away. She didn't think she could bear it if he rejected her. Not as fragile as her emotions were right now. And he'd certainly made it clear at the police station that a future between them would never happen. Was that the truth? Or had he just said that as a defense mechanism, not wanting to open himself up to her again?

He straightened. "Peyton? Did Duncan upset you?"

Yes. "No, of course not. The past twenty-four hours have upset me. I can't seem to find my balance." She tried to smile, wasn't sure that she'd succeeded. "Would it be okay with you if we put off the questions until later?" Thunder boomed, making her wince. "A few hours won't make much of a difference, will they? It's not like anyone can head out searching in this weather, right?"

He hesitated, then nodded. "Of course. A few hours shouldn't hurt. But the storm is supposed to ease later this evening. The trackers will be out looking again. We don't want to wait too long."

"Okay. Thank you." She hurried past him into the house, suddenly in desperate need of some space.

Chapter Nine

The easy camaraderie Peyton had experienced with Colin this morning evaporated as the day wore on, probably because she was still mulling over what Duncan had said. Colin knew something was bothering her. But since she kept denying it, he was becoming more and more reserved. She hated that she was bringing out the stranger again, after having a precious glimpse of the old Colin earlier. But this was something she had to work out for herself.

How could she help her brother and love Colin too? Without hurting either of them?

After an awkward lunch with stilted conversation, Colin shut himself in his office down the back hallway. Peyton had been left to her own devices, which meant that she'd been baking. She'd made so much that she'd called Joan to come take the goods to the shop as soon as there was a break in the storm, rather than let them go to waste. She wouldn't even have to worry about baking more in the morning. The café was set for a while.

But even before calling Joan, Peyton had called her father to check on him and update him on the search for Brian. That had led to her admitting that she'd gotten the information from Colin and that she was temporarily staying at his new house. The ensuing argument had her belatedly wishing that she hadn't even called him. So, when she'd called Joan right after that, it had been a blessing to have that conversation go much better.

Joan had jumped at the chance to work extra shifts and had assured Peyton that Melissa would too, because she was in a tight spot and some extra money would really help out right now. Peyton felt guilty for not offering them the opportunity in the past. She decided that she'd have to give them raises, maybe even a small bonus once she was back at the shop, even if it meant dipping into her meager savings to cover the expense.

When Joan showed up for the baked goods, Colin disabled the alarm and stood guard, making her so nervous that she didn't stay any longer than it took to load her car. Peyton didn't want to speak to him in his current mood either, let alone suffer through another agonizing interview like the one with Landry. But the storm was definitely ending, as Colin had predicted. Putting off his questions was no longer an option. She reluctantly told him she was ready. Several hours later, she was convinced that Landry had been a prince. Colin, on the other hand, was a sadist.

He grilled her over and over with the same questions, rephrasing them, going off on tangents that didn't seem relevant in any way, circling back and asking the same things all over again. He took copious notes, asking her about things Brian had said, texted, emailed, any people he'd ever mentioned that he associated with at the prison. He asked for a list of anyone Brian had ever visited, talked to, or even fought with from the time they were little kids. She'd had to tell Colin all the places her brother loved to go, how often he went there, who went with him. And on and on and on.

Occasionally he'd retreat to his office to call Chief Landry or the marshals assigned to find Brian. She didn't like the idea of them sharing information back and forth. After all, if she and Colin did figure out where Brian was, she wanted Colin to capture him, not some over-anxious police officer. But she had to trust him, and put faith in his years of experience that he'd somehow manage to keep her brother safe.

Even with her fears, she welcomed the times Colin would close himself up in his office. It gave her a break. She came up with her own tactic to stop the questioning every now and then, asking for trips to the bathroom—so many that he'd sarcastically offered to take her to a doctor.

That was the end of her bathroom breaks.

The sun had set long ago by the time they stopped for a late dinner of soup and sandwiches that they prepared together. Working with him in the kitchen to make the food and clean up afterwards was easy, fun. They made a good team. She didn't even mind that they ate without talking. It was better than being endlessly questioned. But, of course, the respite didn't last long. Soon they were back at it again. The Spanish Inquisition had nothing on Deputy US Marshal Colin McKenzie.

She crossed her arms and shifted into a more comfortable position on the couch while she waited for his next question.

He scrolled through the screen on his tablet, checking his notes. "Let's see. You said when Brian began his prison sentence, you visited him once a week. But about a year ago, the visits stopped. Why did you stop visiting him?"

"We argued. He didn't want to see me anymore."

"That's not an answer."

"It's private. It has nothing to do with the escape. I promise. We never discussed him getting out except through legal means—appeals mainly, since parole isn't an option at a federal prison. That's it." She held her hands out. "How did he escape anyway? I don't understand. Shouldn't it be nearly impossible to do that?"

"It should be. But the government sometimes hires out prisoner transportation to private firms to save money. The employees can be overworked, overtired and undertrained. And the vans aren't always maintained as well as they should be. The investigation is ongoing, but it appears that all of those factors contributed to the prisoners being able to pry open a faulty lock and sneak out the back of the van at a fuel stop."

"Wow. That's crazy—scary too. Please tell me that's rare, that people don't escape prison transports every day."

"They don't. But it does happen. This isn't a one-off. Luckily there was no one else around, so no one was hurt at the gas station. They took off on foot, later stole a car that someone had left unlocked with the keys inside."

"Is that how the police officer, Jennings, got involved? He saw them in a stolen car and tried to arrest them?"

"Yes, he..." Colin sighed. "How did we turn the tables here? You're supposed to be answering my questions, not the other way around."

"No one has told me anything. It's really frustrating."

"It's frustrating for all of us. There are a lot of things we still don't know. Like how the prisoners got the gun they used to shoot Officer Jennings."

"I don't have any guns. I can probably shoot better than most people I know because you taught me back when we were dating. But I don't own one, never have. And before you ask, no, I did not somehow provide Brian with a gun."

"Then we're back to the argument you had with him. Maybe it matters, maybe it doesn't. But I'd like to be the judge of that. What did you argue about?"

"You're not going to drop this, are you?"

"No. I'm not."

She shoved her hair back from her face. "You, okay? We argued about you."

He stared at her. "Me?"

"Brian thinks you're the devil, that everything that's happened to him is your fault."

He looked down at the white lines on his hands, his mouth tightening. "What do you think?"

"I think that you're the most honorable person I know. Do I wish that you hadn't testified against him? Yes. But I don't hold it against you. You promised to tell the truth. And I have no doubt that you told the truth as you see it. I don't blame you for anything, Colin."

His gaze flicked to hers. "I appreciate that."

"It's true." She clasped her hands tightly together. "Anyway, I couldn't take Brian's drama anymore. I've tried for years to get him to continue his education behind bars so he'd have a skill when he got out. I'd had a tough week, was struggling to find a new job after getting laid off at my previous one. I guess I kind of exploded. It shocked him. He must have felt betrayed, like he'd lost his biggest ally."

She shrugged. "Maybe our argument did play a role in the escape. Maybe he felt he had nothing left to lose and no one else to trust. I do know that prison was exceptionally hard on him. I mean, he'd have these mental breakdowns, end up in psychiatric treatment for months. You mentioned he had only five more years to serve. To Brian, five more years was an eternity. He was miserable. The whole time. He never adjusted in any way."

"You were his biggest ally? What about your parents?"

She wrapped her arms around her middle. "In the beginning, they saw him weekly, along with me. But something happened a couple of years ago. Dad and Mom had a fight, not that fighting was new for them. They've seen a marriage counselor for as long as I can remember. But this was worse, really bad. Things... changed. Between my parents, and between them and Brian. Dad went to see him one more time, by himself, and never went back. Mom started visiting him on her own, without me. I never understood why. She never told me."

"This blowup happened, your dad stopped seeing his son, your mom started seeing him alone, but no one ever explained what it was all about?"

"It was about Brian. That's a given. Mom always took up for him. Dad was always putting him down, since he was a little boy. Brian's shenanigans while growing up were an embarrassment to him. To my dad, reputation was everything. That's why he fought so hard for Brian, trying to keep him from going to prison. He wanted his son proven innocent so he could salvage the family name. All I can figure is that whatever their recent argument was about, it had to be about something that would embarrass my father even more if it got out."

"Like maybe Brian admitted he really had set the fire?"

She hesitated, then shrugged. "I can't imagine that happening. But, yes, if that was the case, my father would be ashamed and forced to admit he'd been wrong all this time. He can hold his head up now and insist the Sterlings are good, solid people and our family has suffered a tragic injustice. If he was proven wrong, he'd be devasted, bitter, ashamed." She shook her head. "Whatever it was, it tore my parents apart. Mom wouldn't go to marriage counseling anymore unless my dad would visit Brian. He refused. They were at an impasse."

The questions continued. Like any good son of a judge and a prosecutor, he covered the same ground again and again until she wanted to beg for mercy. After answering yet another question that she'd answered many times before, she dropped her head back against the cushy leather couch and closed her eyes. "Couldn't you just waterboard me or something? That would be less torture than this."

"What do you mean?" He sounded genuinely surprised.

She lifted her head. "You're kidding, right?"

He arched a brow.

"You're not kidding. Wow. Okay, we've been going

around and around for hours. You keep asking me the same questions. I keep giving you the same answers. How is this getting us anywhere?"

He glanced at the darkened windows outside, checked his watch. "You're right. I may have overdone it."

"You think?"

"How about one more question?"

"Does the one you just asked count?"

He smiled. "No."

"Fine. One more. Then I turn into a pumpkin. A nontalking pumpkin."

"Some of them talk?"

"Obviously, you go to the wrong pumpkin patches."

"I'll have to remember that. Okay. Final question."

"Final answer. Drumroll, folks." She tapped her hands on her thighs, mimicking a drummer.

"You explained why you stopped visiting Brian. But then, three months ago, you went to see him one more time. Why?"

She closed her eyes. "Last question? Promise?"

"Promise. Unless I have a follow-up related to the original question, of course."

"Of course." She sighed. "It was because of my mom." She gave him a watery smile. "The subject I've been avoiding ever since the police station. I had to tell Brian about Mom. She…there was an accident, a car accident. It was raining. She lost control on a curve and slammed into a tree. The coroner said she died instantly. Thank God. She never felt the flames." She sucked in a breath and glanced at his hands. "I'm sorry. I shouldn't have—"

"It's okay. I'm sorry about your mom, Peyton. I really am."

She blinked furiously, then nodded.

"What about your dad?" he asked, his voice gentle. "Was he hurt in the accident?"

She blew out a deep breath, still feeling awful for bringing up the fire—even though it was in response to his questions. She just wished she'd measured her words more carefully.

"Dad wasn't with her. He's fine. As well as he can be."

"He lives in Memphis? Alone?"

"He does now."

"What do you mean, now? Was someone else living with him until recently?"

"I'm guessing this is one of those follow-up questions?"

He smiled again. "If you don't mind."

"I do mind. But I'll answer anyway. I'd moved out of my dad's place years ago, but...circumstances changed and I moved back. Then, after Mom died, he said he needed some time to figure things out. He needed his space."

"He kicked you out?"

Her stomach churned. She didn't have to ask what he was thinking. She'd practically grown up with the McKenzie family. The idea that their mother or father would turn away one of their four sons was ludicrous. Even amid all the stunts their youngest son, Ian, had pulled, they showed nothing but patience and love for him.

She lifted her chin. "I gave my father the space he needed in order to get over a terrible tragedy."

"You suffered the same tragedy."

"Don't," she warned. "Don't judge my father, or my family."

"I can't pretend to understand your father's actions. But I *am* sorry for your loss. I know you and your mom were close. She was…different. We didn't exactly click. But I respected her, because she loved you."

Was that what he thought? That her mother loved her? Peyton wasn't so sure. She'd always loved her mom and desperately tried to make her mom love her in return. But Peyton was never quite sure whether there was enough room in her mother's heart for anyone besides her beloved son. She forced a smile. "Thank you."

"You're welcome."

"Since you're being so nice, I'll give you a bonus answer without you having to ask another follow-up question. When Dad…asked me to leave, it's not like I didn't have resources. He knew I'd be okay. I have a small inheritance, an investment fund that my parents set up years ago in case anything ever happened to either of them. Plus a small life insurance payout. The house here in Gatlinburg is paid off. It's pretty much the only asset Dad hasn't sold. He's keeping it for after he retires. The point is, I can live here rent free, which helped me allocate my funds towards starting my own business. I figured it would be nice to be my own boss for a change instead of being at the mercy of corporations and budget cuts."

"Corporations? Where did you work?"

"Here and there. Whatever I could do to make ends meet."

"You wanted to work in the criminal justice field the last I knew. What happened to that dream?"

"When everyone in the family is working to pay a lawyer, that kind of nixes any plans to pay for college. Not that I'm complaining. It was my choice to start working right out of high school to help with Brian's legal bills."

He stared at her. "You were eighteen. Too young to throw away your dreams."

She shrugged. "You do what you have to do. Besides, I didn't throw away my dreams. I made new ones. That's why I started my shop. Although I'd give anything to have my mom back, the money she left me was a gift. That's what allowed me a fresh start. It's a struggle, but if I can make the café profitable, I'll have some stability in my life again, something long term. And we both know I love to bake."

"Do you? Are you sure about that?"

"Excuse me?"

"All your life, you've sacrificed for others. You were Brian's protector, his second mom, for as long as I can remember. You didn't go to college because you wanted to help your parents with the legal bills. Now you've started a small business that allows you to employ a couple of women who were unemployable by everyone else."

She fisted her hands in her lap. "You make it sound like helping others is a bad thing."

"It is when you're sacrificing yourself along the way. You talk about money being tight. But according to the investigation Landry has been leading, your shop is extremely successful. You should be in the black, not losing money. After seeing the enormous amount of bread you baked and gave to Joan, I can see why. That wasn't all for the café was it? I'll bet if I call the homeless shelter, I'll find that Peyton's Place is making huge donations of food every single day."

She gritted her teeth. "The soup kitchen," she admitted. "Not the homeless shelter."

"Soup kitchen. So they can feed the homeless and poor. Like I said. That's wonderful, Peyton. It truly is. The rest of us could learn a thing or two from all the good that you do. But what I want to know is—why?"

"Why do I want to help people?"

"Not just why do you want to help people. Why do you help them to the exclusion of yourself? You aren't living your life, Peyton. You're in servitude to others. I bet you're working more now than you did when you worked for corporate America. Why are you killing yourself for everyone else?"

She stared at his hands, at the white lines, before forcing herself to meet his probing gaze. "You wouldn't understand."

"I want to. Explain it to me."

She spread her hands in a helpless gesture. "Someone else starts a fire and you, Colin McKenzie, run into that burning building and save lives. Do you know how rare that is? For someone to be that selfless?"

"Peyton, I'm not—"

"Selfless? Yes. You are. You're so good, Colin. You're why I wanted to go into the criminal justice field all those years ago, you and your amazing family. Every one of you has made a career out of helping others. And then—" she shook her head "—then there's *my* family. I grew up watching my father pay people off to clean up Brian's messes." She grimaced. "Fights, graffiti, things like that. From what Chief Landry said at the station, it appears Brian did a lot more than I'd ever realized as a child. My mom, God love her, she wasn't just eccentric. She was a space cadet. And she played favorites with her children. It's one of the reasons that she and Dad fought so much. He loved me. She loved Brian. With no in between." A tear slid down her cheek. She furiously wiped it away.

"Everything for her was about Brian. There was never any time for me. That's why I started baking. Not because I wanted to, but because Mom loved to bake. That was the only time she seemed proud of me, happy with me. It was the only time she loved *me*."

"Peyton, stop. You don't have to—"

She held up her hands. "No. Let me finish. I'm not trying to play a blame game here and paint my parents in a bad light. We all made mistakes, huge mistakes. I was probably the worst offender, always protecting my brother when I should have been making him stand on his own two feet. He's always been different, eccentric, I guess, like you said about my mom. They were so alike. But I was an enabler, just as much as my dad every time he used money to make one of Brian's problems go away. You're like your father, William, The Mighty McKenzie, fighting for truth and justice. That's your legacy. What's mine? I'm a Sterling, with a dysfunctional family and an escaped convict for a brother. And, and…"

Colin moved to the couch beside her, taking one of her hands in his. She clutched it, unable to refuse the lifeline he offered.

She wiped at her tears again. "The more you ask me questions, the more I'm learning about this case, the more I'm scared to death that Brian may have started that damn fire after all." She clutched his hand harder. "You ask me why I'm using every penny I can to employ two women who wouldn't have jobs otherwise. Or why I make up repair work so I can feed a homeless man without him feeling like it's charity." She pressed her fist against her heart. "Because I'm scared to death that I'm like my father, my mother, my brother. I'm a Sterling by name. But not here." She pounded her chest. "Not in my heart. I don't want *their* legacy to be *my* legacy. I want to be a good person, Colin." She tapped her fist against her heart with each word she said. "I need to be a good person."

He gently brushed her hair back from her face. "Peyton. You are a good person. You always have been."

She shook her head. "No. I'm not. I should have been there for you, after the fire. No matter what my dad told me. Even if he did lock my door, take away my stupid phone. I should have been there."

His eyes widened.

"I should have found a way," she continued, the words feeling as if they were being ripped from her soul. "Duncan said you needed me, but I wasn't there. I wasn't there." She collapsed against him, sobbing so hard she could barely draw a breath.

He swore and scooped her up, cradling her against his chest. He carried her upstairs and tucked her into the guest bed, whispering soothing words the whole time. The day's emotional toll had her so exhausted she struggled to open her eyes.

"Shh," he whispered. "It's okay, Peyton. Don't worry about anything. It's all going to be okay."

She fell asleep to the gentle pressure of his kiss against her forehead.

Chapter Ten

Drowning in guilt and self-loathing, Colin fisted his hands and paced back and forth in his bedroom downstairs. He couldn't shake the image of Peyton's beautiful, pixie-like face wet with tears. Her sweet, gentle voice choked with raw, gut-wrenching pain.

I don't want their legacy to be my legacy. I want to be a good person.

A good person? She was the *epitome* of good. The entire time he'd known her, she'd done things for other people, always putting them first. It was one of the reasons he'd fallen in love with her. She was the kindest, most caring person he'd ever met. And it had never occurred to him, until tonight, that her gentle, selfless nature hid a sea of pain.

I should have been there for you, after the fire.

Yes. But he should have been there for her too. He should have fought for her, realized something was keeping her from being at his side. Instead, he'd been so hurt, so consumed by his own pain and the giant-sized chip on his shoulder that he'd never once considered that she might be hurting. That maybe she needed him too.

What lies had her father told to keep them apart?

She'd mentioned him locking her up, taking away her phone. Had his goal been specifically to isolate her from Colin? Had he told her Colin's injuries weren't significant or that he didn't want to see her? She'd been young, naive in many ways. They both had. Colin could easily imagine her being manipulated by her father, using her fierce protectiveness toward her brother as a means to control her.

As she'd said tonight, the fact that her father hadn't been close to his son didn't mean he wouldn't fight for Brian. Benjamin Sterling's reputation, his family's reputation, his business reputation as a trusted financial advisor, had all been at stake. If he'd seen Colin as the enemy, because his testimony could send Brian to prison and hurt his business, Colin could easily imagine him doing everything he could to stop him—including using his own daughter. The elder Sterling had wanted a united family front behind Brian. And he'd probably hoped, planned, that Colin would be so distraught over not being able to see Peyton, and worried about hurting her, that he might not testify.

His plan had almost worked.

At eighteen, Colin's entire life had been centered around the beautiful strawberry blonde with the sexy smile and silver-gray eyes that made promises his body was only too willing to take her up on. When she cut him out of his life, it had nearly destroyed him. Only the love and support of his tight-knit family had gotten him through. Ultimately, a stern lecture about civic responsibility from his father, William—known in legal circles as The Mighty McKenzie—had been the only reason that he'd persevered and kept it together long enough to testify. He'd done his duty, sitting upright in the witness stand, his face carefully blank, pretending that he wasn't in excruciating pain. After walking out of the courtroom, he'd collapsed, and ended up in the hospital for another month.

The combination of his injuries and the belief that Peyton had willingly dumped him had sent him on a downward spiral. But he'd never considered that Brian's treachery, and her father's duplicity, had done the same to her.

Even later, after finding out that she'd gotten married, he'd assumed life was great for her. Well she didn't seem to have a husband now and wasn't wearing a ring. But he'd never bothered to ask if she was okay, if she'd suffered through a divorce or went through the trauma of losing her husband in some kind of accident or illness. Instead, he'd chosen to assume her life was all roses, that she was doing whatever she wanted, making friends, living a carefree life. In reality, she'd been working herself ragged going from job to job to help pay her brother's legal bills, while Colin had nursed his hurt feelings and congratulated himself on being the better person.

What an arrogant ass he'd been.

That wasn't his only sin against her. The supposed deal he'd made with her at the police station was a farce. Arresting her was never something he'd considered. The charges never would have stuck, as Landry knew, or he'd have arrested her himself. Then Colin had compounded his lies by exaggerating the danger to Brian.

His brothers in arms weren't a bunch of Mayberries who shot first and asked questions later. They were experienced professionals, intent on recapturing—not killing—four escaped convicts. He'd known the search for Brian and the others was in competent hands, which was why he'd been comfortable exchanging information with them. But he'd allowed Peyton to stew in worry, using that fear to make her answer his questions.

He shook his head in disgust and stopped pacing. All this self-recrimination wasn't doing him, or Peyton, any good. He owed her a heartfelt apology. But waking her up at midnight when she'd cried herself into an exhausted sleep would be one more selfish act to lay at his door. He wouldn't do it. But he had to do *something* with all this guilt and nervous energy or he was going to explode.

He moved to the window and looked out past the covered, wraparound porch. A gentle breeze rippled across the lawn, making the rain-wet blades of grass sparkle in the moonlight. The grass was a bit ragged and higher than he liked to keep it. His lawn tractor had broken down a couple of weeks ago and he hadn't had time to fix it. Sweating and struggling with that stubborn tractor engine was infinitely preferable to wrestling with his conscience. He could change the oil in the ATVs he kept in the workshop building too. Might as well do something productive if he wasn't going to sleep.

He figured the odds of Brian and his fellow thugs heading up the mountain and being anywhere near this place were low. Without knowing that Colin had a house here, or that Peyton was with him, there was no reason for her brother to risk being caught by remaining in the immediate area. Besides that, Officer Simmons was staying at the Sterling home for now. If she'd seen anything suspicious, she'd have called him. Still, it wouldn't hurt to take precautions.

He dressed as if he was going to work, making sure his gun was loaded and holstered at his hip with two extra magazines of ammunition in his pocket. It wasn't unusual for the occasional black bear to wander onto the property and it was best to be prepared. He grabbed a flashlight before heading out back.

Except for the well-used charcoal grill and a couple of lounge chairs, his back deck was empty. No muddy shoe prints marred the surface to indicate any recent visitors. He jogged down the steps into the yard, stopping at the tool shed fifty yards from the house. A circuit around the perimeter with his flashlight didn't reveal any tracks other than some paw prints that had likely been left by a hungry raccoon searching for its next meal. The padlock was securely in place on the door. The shed didn't have any windows.

He swept the beam of his flashlight back and forth along the trees that bordered two sides of the property. But aside from low-hanging branches gracefully moving in the steady, warm breeze, there wasn't any unexplained movement or shadows that didn't look like they belonged. Satisfied that all was well, he clicked off the flashlight and used the light of the moon to guide him toward his workshop. He was ten feet from his destination when the little hairs stood up on the back of his neck.

Chapter Eleven

Peyton bolted out of bed and fell to the floor, her legs tangled in the sheets. She batted at the stubborn material to free herself as she scanned the dark recesses of the bedroom. No bogeyman waited to pounce on her from the shadows. But something had startled her awake. What was it?

A small sliver of light leaked beneath the bedroom door. Was Colin still awake? She pushed herself up off the floor and checked the time on her phone, which was charging on the nightstand. A little past midnight. Maybe he was catching an old movie or watching a rerun of a favorite college basketball game. He'd always been a Tennessee Vols fan and had hoped to go to the University of Tennessee after high school. Had he gone? She hadn't thought to ask him.

Maybe he was having a late-night snack. Or, more likely after her humiliating outburst earlier tonight, he was regretting having his crazy ex-girlfriend around and was trying to think of a polite way to get rid of her. She certainly wouldn't blame him.

Bam!

She jerked back, swearing when her shin slammed against the wooden bedframe. *What was that?*

Bam! Bam!

She sucked in a breath. Gunshots. Coming from outside, behind the house.

She hesitated, not sure what to do, half-expecting Colin to burst into the bedroom to check on her. When he didn't, a nagging sense of unease released a firestorm of butterflies in her stomach. She grabbed her phone, fingers poised to punch in his number—but she didn't *have* his number, or Duncan's or any of the McKenzies. Not anymore.

Clutching the phone, she ran to the closet to throw on some clothes. She yanked on a pair of jeans and a shirt, not bothering with a bra. After shoving her feet into some tennis shoes, she took off running. She practically flew down the stairs, hopping down them two at a time, a feat she'd never have thought possible before tonight, since she wasn't blessed with long legs like Colin.

The big-screen TV hanging on the far wall of the family room wasn't on. The light she'd seen from upstairs was coming from the back hallway. She hopped off the bottom step and circled around to the rear of the house. Her sense of unease intensified when she discovered that the lights in his office were on too, but the office was empty. A quick peek behind the other doors in the hall revealed a bathroom, a closet and the laundry room, but no sign of Colin.

"Colin? Colin? Are you here? Are you okay?" She yelled for him as she ran toward his bedroom at the front of the house. All the while she prayed that he'd yank open his door and look at her as if he thought she'd lost her mind. That would be infinitely better than the alternative, that he was outside where she'd heard those gunshots. But when she reached his door it was standing wide open. She didn't have to flip on the light to see that his bed was empty, looking as if it hadn't been slept in.

"Colin?" Her voice came out a hoarse whisper. The butterflies degenerated into full-blown panic as she ran through the house to the last place he could be, the kitchen. Just as she'd feared, it too was empty.

Boom! Boom!

She dropped to the floor, her pulse rushing in her ears. That had sounded so close!

Please, please don't let that be Brian out there shooting at Colin.

Her nerdy, insecure brother wasn't someone she'd ever thought could hurt someone. But as Landry had reminded her earlier, Brian did know how to shoot, almost as well as Peyton. Colin had taught both of them. Was Brian out there right now? Shooting at the man who'd been so patient with him when they were teenagers, and far kinder than most kids at school had been to her socially awkward brother?

Listening to Colin's theories and being forced to reevaluate every facet of her life—and Brian's—had opened jagged cracks in her confidence, letting the first stirrings of doubt creep in about his innocence—or guilt. Even if her long-held beliefs about Brian were still valid, she had no illusions about the men who'd escaped with him. One of them had murdered a police officer. They probably wouldn't think twice about killing a marshal.

Drawing a bracing breath, she forced herself to stop

cowering and look out the window. A yellow bug light cast a warm glow across the deck. Beyond that, there was only darkness and the looming silhouette of a building that resembled a small barn. Had Colin taken his gun with him and gone outside to confront someone he'd seen sneaking around his property? Or had he already been outside, maybe without a gun at all, when the shooting started?

She yanked her phone out of her pocket, berating herself for not making this call as soon as she'd heard the first shot.

"Nine-one-one, what's your emergency?" a woman's voice came on the line.

"This is Peyton Sterling. I'm at Deputy US Marshal Colin McKenzie's home." She rattled off the address. "I can't find him. He was in the house earlier. But now he's gone. I heard gunshots out back. I think he's in trouble. It's possible that the escaped convicts everyone's been looking for are here and they're—"

"Ma'am, Ms. Sterling, hold it. I need you to slow down. You said you heard gunshots?"

"Get the police out here immediately, and an ambulance just in case. Send the marshals, send everyone. Colin needs help!" She tossed the phone on the counter, tuning out the operator's barrage of useless questions.

Bam! Boom! Boom!

Muzzle flashes appeared in the woods off to the left. There was no answering flash in the yard, but earlier she'd thought she heard return gunfire. If that had been Colin, then he was either inside the barn-like building firing from a window, or he was on the other side, possibly pinned down and unable to get to safety. He needed backup. Now. Not in twenty minutes, or however long it would take the police to climb up that crazy winding road out front. The only person around to be his backup was her. She swallowed and rubbed her palms against her jeans. What she really needed right now was a huge dose of courage.

And a gun.

Think, Peyton. Think. If you lived here, where would you keep an extra gun and ammunition? It would be some place easy to get to in case an intruder broke in. But not where a child or casual visitor would stumble across it.

She whirled around and her gaze locked on the pantry door. Colin put his coffee mugs where she kept hers. Would he put a gun and ammo where she'd keep hers too, easy to grab, close to an exit in case she had to run outside to either pursue or run from a bad guy?

She jogged into the pantry, throwing open the door so hard that it banged against the wall. Then she flipped the light switch and looked up. There—a wooden box on the top shelf. Just the right size to store a weapon. It was too high for small children to reach. Which meant it was too high for her too.

Bouncing on her tiptoes, she jumped up and down, desperately stretching her fingers up, up, up. She stumbled and fell against the shelving, barely managing to stay upright.

"Dang it, Colin. Why do you have to be so tall?"

She whirled around, looking for a ladder or a step stool, cursing herself for wasting time when she didn't find any. Colin wouldn't need them to reach the top shelf. So what could she use? A chair. But he didn't have a dining room where she could grab one. There wasn't even a table in the kitchen.

But there were bar stools.

She ran to the kitchen island and dragged one of the bar stools into the pantry, wincing at the sound of the metal legs scraping the hardwood floor.

Boom! Bam! Bam!

The sound of fresh gunfire sent her flying up on the bar stool like a monkey and grabbing the wooden box. She jumped down and tried to flip open the top. It wouldn't budge. The dang thing was locked!

She cried out in frustration. Of course it was locked. Colin was a marshal. He wouldn't take any chances that someone might get hold of one of his guns and hurt themselves. It looked sophisticated too, one of those fancy electronic boxes that required a fingerprint to open it.

Using curse words she hadn't realized were in her vocabulary, she scrambled to her feet and grabbed a large can off a nearby shelf. English peas. She hated peas. She raised the can and brought it crashing down. Again. Again. Again. Wood splintered and crunched. The lock held. The box didn't. She kissed the can, deciding she liked peas after all.

Lying on a bed of red velvet dusted by bits of ruined wood was the prettiest sight she'd ever seen. A Glock 22, the .40 caliber pistol framed by two full magazines. How many times had she complained when Colin insisted on taking her shooting in the mountains, sometimes with her brother tagging along? She'd assured him that her career path in the criminal justice field wouldn't be the same as his, that she'd be a victim's advocate or a defense attorney, not a cop. She didn't need to know how to fire a gun.

He would tell her it wasn't about her career. It was about making sure the woman he loved could protect herself in a world that too often was cruel and dangerous, especially for women. Well, tonight it was dangerous for men. One man in particular.

She shoved one of the magazines into the pistol and chambered a round. Pocketing the other magazine, she lunged to her feet.

"You've done everything you could to protect me, Colin. Now it's my turn to protect you."

Chapter Twelve

Colin crouched down, his left shoulder butted up against the workshop building as he pointed his .40 caliber Glock 22 toward the woods to the south of his property. In spite of there being no physical evidence that anyone was out here when he'd reached the building, his instincts had told him something was off. He'd cleared the inside, then made a circuit around the perimeter. He'd just reached the far side of the building when the first shot had kicked up the dirt beside him. Since then, he'd been pinned down in this same spot.

The solid wall on this side of the structure offered no access to the inside. And the shooter, or shooters, were having fun at his expense. They were aiming their shots at the ground, or above his head, forcing him to stay where he was. It was only a matter of time before they tired of their sadistic game and made their shots count.

He had to get out of here.

He eased back toward the corner as he'd tried twice before. This time, he measured his stride in inches, going as slowly as possible, hoping they wouldn't realize he was backing up until it was too late to stop him. One inch, two, three—

Boom! Boom!

He swore and jumped away from the rain of wood and sawdust above and behind him. Laughter sounded from the trees. Familiar laughter? Was that Brian, hiding like the coward he was? Once again playing God with other peoples' lives?

This cat-and-mouse game would end as soon as his tormentors got bored. He couldn't risk waiting any longer. He had to make a run for it, take his chances, lay some heavy cover fire so he could try to get to relative safety. And after that? If the gunmen decided to circle around, get him in their sights again? That was a worst-case scenario he didn't want to think about.

He popped out his empty magazine and shoved in another one. It was now or never. He aimed directly toward where he'd seen the last muzzle flash. *Bam, bam, bam, bam!* He squeezed the trigger over and over, never stopping, emptying the magazine as he backed up.

Boom!

A guttural scream sounded from the woods.

He slammed his last magazine of ammo into the gun and fired again, ducking and weaving, scrambling back toward the corner.

Boom!

The bullet slammed into him like a battering ram, stealing his breath, sending a shockwave of blinding pain through his entire body. He managed to squeeze off two more rounds then dove around the end of the building. He landed on his side and rolled onto his back, clutching at his chest, desperately struggling to get his lungs working again.

"Colin! Oh no, Colin!"

He jerked his head to the side. *Peyton! No!* She leaped from the back deck to the ground and started running toward him, ducking down but still an open, easy target if the gunmen noticed her.

Down! His mind screamed but he couldn't force any words past his constricted throat. *Get down!* He signaled for her to drop to the ground as he gasped like a fish on dry land, mouth open but no air getting in. Blackness hovered at the edge of his vision. No! He had to stay conscious. He had to get her to cover before the gunmen saw her.

Can't pass out. Breathe, damn it. Breathe!

He motioned again for her to get down. She hesitated, then started forward. He flipped onto his stomach and drove his fists against his belly. The impact loosened his diaphragm. Blessed air rushed into his lungs. He gulped it in, ruthlessly fighting back the darkness. He scrambled up, fell against the building, pushed himself upright. He took a wobbly step toward her, another.

She slowed again, then stopped thirty feet away. What was she doing?

"Run!" he rasped, still barely able to talk. He sucked in another lungful of air. "Run!"

Boom! Boom! Shots sounded from the woods again. But Colin couldn't tell where they were aiming.

He brought up his gun to fire back but she was already turning toward the woods, clasping a pistol he hadn't realized she was carrying. *Bam, bam, bam, bam, bam!* She kept squeezing off shots.

Colin holstered his pistol and sprinted toward her. When he reached her she stopped shooting, eyes wide with surprise. He scooped her up in his arms and raced back to the workshop building. As soon as they were behind the wall, he groaned at the painful throbbing in his chest and slid to the grass with her on his lap. The gunshots stopped and the woods went silent. He didn't know if that was good or bad.

"You crazy woman," he gritted out, drawing a shallow breath to try to ease the pain. "What were you thinking? You could have been killed."

"So could you! You shouldn't have left your cover to come get me."

He stared at her in disbelief. "I shouldn't have... I shouldn't have." He shook his head. "You scared ten years off my life, Peyton. If you ever do something like that again, I swear..." He yanked her against him, hugging her fiercely, not caring that it hurt like hell.

"Can't. Breathe. Colin," she choked out.

He let her go. "Sorry. Good grief, you scared me." He shook his head and scrubbed his face, then winced and rubbed his chest.

"Ditto." She put her left hand on his shoulder, the Glock still clutched in her right hand, finger on the frame instead of the trigger, the gun pointed away from him. Just as he'd taught her so many years ago. If he hadn't still been so rattled, he'd have told her he was proud of how well she'd handled the gun, was still handling it.

"What happened to you?" she asked. "I heard gunshots. Saw you leap around the corner of the building and then you were rolling on the ground."

"Had the wind knocked out of me. Took a bullet, dead center to the chest. The bastards."

She drew a sharp breath, eyes wide as she looked

him up and down. "I don't see any blood. Where's the entrance wound?"

"The round hit me in the vest. I wasn't really expecting trouble, but came prepared, dressed just as I would for work, just in case." He shifted, then winced.

"A vest," she choked out. "You're wearing a vest. Thank God." She let out a shuddering breath. "When I heard the gunshots, saw you fall…" She shook her head.

"Why in the world would you run outside if you heard gunshots?" he demanded.

She looked at him as if she thought he'd lost his mind. "Because they were shooting at you! You needed backup."

"You're a civilian. Not backup. You shouldn't have risked your life like that."

"You're kidding, right? Colin, you were—"

"Where did you get the gun?"

"It's yours, from the pantry." She bit her bottom lip. "I had to smash the box it was in to get the pistol out. It looked nice, expensive."

"I don't care about a stupid box. I care about *you*." He pulled her against him again, less tightly this time, ignoring the fresh wave of pain in his bruised chest. Since she was hugging him back, the pain was well worth it.

Sirens sounded from down the mountain, coming up fast. He froze, then set her away from him and looked toward the house. Although he couldn't see the road out front, the lights from approaching emergency vehicles lit the night sky in hues of red, orange, and blue.

"You called the police?"

"Of course. I wasn't sure that you and I would be able to hold off whoever was shooting at you." Her eyes widened in dismay. "I should have called that officer at my house. It didn't even occur to me! She was much closer."

"You did great." He searched her gaze. "Did you realize your brother could be one of the shooters?"

She looked away, her chin wobbling, and gave him a sharp nod. He realized she was close to losing her composure. She'd known that Brian might be out there, in the woods. But she'd called the police anyway, and risked her own life, not to protect her brother this time, but to protect Colin.

She twisted her hands together, drew a ragged breath. "Did you see who was shooting at you? Do you…do you know if—"

"I didn't see anyone." He coaxed her hands apart, held them in his. "Try not to worry. We'll find out soon enough who was out there."

The sirens were louder now, probably a few hundred yards from the driveway. She turned the pistol around and offered it to him. "You'd better take this. If the cops see a Sterling with a gun, they'll probably shoot first and ask questions later."

"I think you're doing Gatlinburg PD a disservice in thinking that. But I understand where you're coming from." He shoved the pistol into his waistband, then cupped her face between his hands.

Her silver-gray eyes caught the moonlight as she stared at him in surprise.

He shouldn't kiss her. It would be a mistake on so many levels. But he also knew there was no way he could *not* kiss her at that moment. Her selfless act humbled him to the core and reminded him of the hundred different reasons he'd loved her. Still loved her. Maybe, just maybe, there could be a future between them again, once all of this was settled.

He pulled her to him, slowly, gently, giving her plenty of time to stop him if she wanted. But she didn't. Instead, her eyes fluttered closed, her breath tumbling out of her on a soft sigh. He knew he was lost the moment his lips touched hers. Electricity shot through every nerve ending, firing to life again as if reawakening after being in hibernation for a very, very long time. His hands shook as he molded her luscious body to his, drinking her into his starved senses. She trembled in his arms and kissed him back with an equally wild abandon, as if she too couldn't get enough of him.

All too soon, shouts and loud voices broke into the passionate haze that had wrapped around them. Bright lights flashed against his closed eyelids. He reluctantly broke the kiss and turned to see police officers and firefighters running around both sides of his house like ants pouring out of an anthill. Powerful flashlight beams danced across the ground, across the workshop building, across Peyton and him.

He sighed and looked back at Peyton. Her gorgeous eyes were unfocused, passion warring with wonder and surprise. She licked her lips.

His body tightened with need.

"Colin." Her gaze dropped to his mouth. "I wish—"

"Over here!" someone yelled. "There's a body in the woods!"

Her eyes widened. "Brian!" She scrambled off his lap and ran toward one of the policemen approaching them.

Colin recognized him as Patrick Edwards, an excellent officer he'd worked with numerous times over the years whenever one of his taskforces partnered with the Gatlinburg police. Peyton didn't seem to notice that the officer's hand inched closer to his holster as she approached.

"It's okay, Patrick," Colin called out. "She's a witness. She saved my life."

Patrick's eyebrows rose in surprise but he nodded and relaxed his hand. He smiled at Peyton, giving her a polite nod when she stopped in front of him gesturing excitedly as she no doubt asked about her brother.

Now that his brief but pleasant interlude with Peyton was over, Colin's bruised chest decided it was time to remind him that it wasn't happy about being ignored. He closed his eyes and tried to take shallow breaths. Somehow the pain seemed worse now than when he'd first been hit. Probably because he'd been moving around too much.

"I can't believe you kissed her."

He sighed and opened his eyes. Duncan frowned down at him, hands on hips.

"You saw that, huh?"

"Half the police force did and a handful of firefighters."

Colin groaned. "Help me up."

Duncan shook his head and motioned toward some EMTs who'd just rounded the garage end of the house and seemed confused about where to go. "Since you're sitting on your butt instead of jumping into the fray with everyone else running around your property, I'm guessing you're hurt."

"Just bruised. Took a bullet in the vest."

"Let me guess. It only hurts when you breathe?"

"Pretty much." He held his hand out and this time Duncan hauled him to his feet.

The EMTs rushed up to him, two wide-eyed young kids who looked like they should be at home with their moms and dads, catching a few more hours of sleep before heading to school in the morning.

"Sir," the shorter one said. "Please sit down and let us check your injuries. Miss Sterling said you'd been shot and needed medical attention."

Colin arched a brow, looking around for her but she'd disappeared. "She did?"

"Yes, sir. Officer Edwards radioed us to come around back."

They both reached for him as if they thought he was about to fall down.

He shoved their hands away. "For the love of… I'm okay. I'm wearing a vest."

They exchanged a confused glance.

"Kevlar? Bullet resistant?"

"Oh," the same guy said. "Well, uh, you could have broken ribs or internal bleeding. We should still check it out, take you to the hospital."

"Hold that thought." He tugged Duncan a few yards away and turned his back to the overeager children. "Did you see where Peyton went?"

Duncan crossed his arms. "Landry was marching her toward your house when I walked up, no doubt to cross-examine her about whatever happened out here. What *did* happen?"

"I got in a gunfight with one or more cowards shooting at me from the woods. I didn't see them, so I'm not sure who—"

"Sir." The second EMT had found his voice. "We need you to sit—"

"Just a minute," he and Duncan both said at the same time.

Another commotion had them turning to see a group of men topping the small rise on the south side of his yard. Three were wearing white lab coats. The rest were police officers, escorting them toward a fifty-foot section of tree line that was being cordoned off with yellow crime scene tape that read DO NOT CROSS.

"The coroner's here. Must have already been close by," Colin said. "There's a body in the woods, one of the shooters. I need to know if it's Brian."

"Couldn't happen to a nicer guy."

"Duncan, I'm not the only one who fired a gun into those woods tonight. Peyton heard the gunshots when she was inside the house, got one of my pistols and ran out in the middle of a gunfight to help me. She not only put her own life on the line, she fired at the gunmen even though her brother could have been one of them."

Duncan paled. "Then she could have—"

"Killed her own brother. To save me. You and I both know that no one in charge is going to concern themselves with allaying her fears. It could be hours before she finds out the truth. I don't want her agonizing and wondering about her brother's fate if I can find out and save her some grief."

"What do you need me to do? Make Landry back off?"

"I need you to run interference with these guys." He motioned behind him, toward the EMTs.

"You got it."

"Thanks, man. I owe you."

Duncan grinned. "And I won't let you forget it." He stepped around Colin. "Gentlemen, let's chat about Kevlar for a minute—"

Colin took off toward the woods. Each step jarred his aching ribs, making him wonder if the EMTs were right and he'd broken something. But finding out would have to wait.

Although Colin didn't have his badge handy, several of the officers recognized him. After explaining that he wanted to see whoever'd been trying to kill him tonight, they allowed him to step under the crime scene tape.

Battery-operated lights were being set up in this section of the woods, making it seem more like midday than a few hours before sunup. The coroner and his assistants were bending over the dead man's body. Colin's above-average height allowed him to see over most of the police standing around. But the dead man was facing away from him.

As he stepped back and moved around the outer perimeter to get a better vantage point, he noted the location of the body in relation to the workshop building. The man would have had a direct line of sight to where Colin had been pinned down. But close-set oaks formed a solid wall to his right, completely blocking the view of the rest of the yard. There was no way that Peyton could have shot him. Which meant that Colin had.

When he finally got a good look at the man's face, he sucked in a sharp breath. Hauntingly familiar silver-gray eyes stared sightlessly back at him. Any hope he'd had of rekindling the relationship between him and Peyton was as dead as the man on the ground.

There was no way Peyton would ever forgive him for this.

Chapter Thirteen

Peyton rested her elbow on the arm of the couch, only half-listening to Chief Landry's questions. The interrogation thing was becoming almost routine. At least this time he didn't intimidate her. After she'd endured hours of questioning by Colin, Landry seemed like a lightweight.

The man was definitely more aggressive in his questioning than he'd been before. She had to give him credit for that. But she still felt that Colin could teach him a thing or two about interviewing techniques. Landry was probably just trying to reassert his authority after she'd ignored his order to sit on the couch when they'd first come inside. Instead, she'd gone upstairs, put on her bra, and brushed her teeth and her hair before coming back down. No way was she going to sit there being stared at by half a dozen men while wondering if they were ogling her braless breasts through her thin white shirt.

"Miss Sterling?" Landry asked. "Do you need me to repeat the question? Maybe you could use a drink or something? I know you've been through an ordeal tonight."

She blinked and realized she'd zoned out again.

Landry's face mirrored more concern than annoyance. Maybe he wasn't as bad as she'd thought. The men and women working for him seemed to like him. And he never raised his voice with them, not that she'd seen so far. He had a kind face, with character. He reminded her a little of her grandfather on her daddy's side when he'd still been alive.

As soon as she realized she was comparing the chief of police to her dearly departed grandpa, she realized just how exhausted she must be. She curled her legs beneath her and stared past the sea of detectives with their tablets and pads of paper toward the windows on the side of the house. Where was Colin? Was he still outside? Had he gone into the woods to figure out how many people had been shooting at him tonight?

Had he discovered the identity of the body that had been found?

No, she couldn't think about that. Every time she did, she started to shake and her throat tightened. It was humiliating enough already, being constantly treated like a criminal when she was just the sister of one. Crying in front of these men was *not* an option. She had to keep it together.

It wasn't Brian. The dead body in the woods wasn't her brother. She had to believe that.

Maybe Colin wasn't outside at all. She'd asked that nice police officer to get him medical help. Not being all that familiar with how bulletproof vests worked, she wasn't sure what kind of damage a shot could cause. But Colin had definitely seemed uncomfortable, to say the least. She imagined he'd be sporting a rainbow of colors on his chest for weeks as the bruises rose to the surface.

"Miss Sterling." The chief's voice broke through her musings again. "Did you hear my question?"

She cleared her throat. "No, sorry. I didn't. Can you tell me where Deputy US Marshal McKenzie is? He was hurt in the gunfight. He was wearing a bulletproof vest but I could tell he was in pain. Is he on the way to the hospital for X-rays or something?"

One of his bushy white eyebrows raised. "McKenzie? Seems like I remember Officer Edwards telling me that he'd sent some EMTs to check on him. I'm sure he's fine. You mentioned you took a pistol from the kitchen and—"

"You're *sure* Colin's fine?" She curled her fingers against the arm of the couch. "Does that mean you don't actually *know*?"

A flash of impatience crossed Landry's face as he turned to the detective beside him. "Get me a status on Deputy Marshal McKenzie. Edwards should be able to help you."

"And my brother." Her voice broke and she had to clear it before continuing. "I need to know whether Brian Sterling was…found on the property. I need to know whether anyone has seen him tonight."

"Peyton."

She turned to see Colin standing by the island that separated the kitchen from the family room.

"Colin!" She jumped up from the couch.

The chief grabbed her hand to keep her from leaving. "Miss Sterling. We aren't through here."

She shook him off. "Yes. We are." She jogged across the family room and would have thrown her arms around Colin in relief that he was okay, except that his chalky-looking face reminded her that he wasn't.

"Oh, Colin. You're so pale. You must be in terrible pain. What did the EMTs say was wrong? Shouldn't you be at the hospital? Where do you keep the medicine around here? I can get you some ibuprofen. If you don't have any, I should have some in my—"

"Peyton. We need to talk." He looked over the top of her head. "Alone. In my office." He took her hand and tugged her with him through the family room, around the couch grouping.

Landry stood and started toward them. "Marshal McKenzie, I'm in the middle of interviewing Miss Sterling. I need to ask you some questions as well."

"It can wait."

His tone brooked no argument. The chief stopped and fell silent as they passed. But the thunderous look on his face told Peyton just how furious he was. She didn't look forward to answering more of his questions.

Colin didn't seem to care one whit about Landry's anger. He completely ignored him as he turned down the back hall, his long strides forcing Peyton to jog to keep up with him.

She'd never seen him like this before. His profile looked etched in stone. His jaw was clamped so tight that the skin whitened along his jawline. Dread settled in her belly, making the earlier butterflies seem tame in comparison. Every instinct inside her told her to run, far away, that she didn't want to hear whatever it was that he was about to tell her.

He shoved the office door open and pulled her inside. A massive glass-and-wrought-iron desk sat in front of the window with two wing chairs across from it. A black leather love seat that matched the couches in the family room backed up against a wall of bookshelves on the left side of the room. He closed and locked the door, then pulled her to the love seat.

"Sit down, Peyton."

She stared up at him. "Colin, I don't—"

"Please."

She slowly lowered herself to the love seat and perched on the edge, her hands clasped together. He sat close beside her and covered her hands with his own. His thumb gently stroked across their fingers, his gaze downcast, his throat working as if he was struggling to find the right words to destroy her world.

In spite of her vow not to cry, a single tear escaped and traced down her cheek. "It's Brian, isn't it?" she said in a hoarse whisper. "Just say it, Colin. The wondering is driving me crazy."

He lifted his head.

She gasped at the raw pain in their stormy blue depths. "No. Oh, no. Brian."

His expression turned to anguish. "I went into the woods, saw the body myself. I had to be sure."

"Then Brian is—"

"No. The man who died tonight wasn't Brian. It was your father. And I'm the one who killed him."

Chapter Fourteen

Colin leaned against one of the posts on his front porch, watching the sun coming up over the mountains, and Peyton driving *down* the mountain in her banged-up white Ford Escape that had definitely seen better days.

A few minutes later, Duncan pulled his work Jeep to a halt in front of the garage. He hopped out and crossed to the porch, propping one of his boots against the bottom step. "Did I just pass Peyton?"

"You probably did. It's Wednesday, for goodness sakes. The middle of the week. Don't you ever work anymore?"

"I could say the same about you."

"I'm still on vacation."

"And I've been falling asleep at my desk with nothing to do since the park is still locked up tight. When are your fellow marshals going to do *their* jobs and catch Brian and his co-thugs so things can get back to normal?"

"I doubt they'll ever get back to normal," Colin mumbled.

"What did you say?"

"Nothing."

"Uh-huh." Duncan motioned down the road. "I don't recall seeing her SUV in your pristine garage when I stopped by the day after the shooting."

"Landry had to finally accept that Brian wasn't dumb enough to return to the Sterling household, so he sent Officer Simmons packing. He had a couple of his men bring Peyton's SUV up here so she could drive home when she was ready."

"I don't remember Landry being that accommodating in the past."

"He usually isn't," Colin agreed. "But after Peyton called 911 even though she knew her brother could have been the one shooting at me, and she risked her life trying to save me, she won over the hearts of a lot of law-enforcement guys around here, including the chief. Plus, I think he feels bad for her since she lost her father. He mentioned that she reminds him of his youngest granddaughter."

"Landry procreated. Who knew? Hey, speaking of dear old Dad, have you and Peyton worked through that?"

Colin shifted against the post, grimacing when his ribs sent up a jolt of pain in protest. At least they were only bruised, as the X-rays had confirmed. That was one thing to be thankful for. "Peyton claims she doesn't blame me for what happened."

"Claims? You don't believe her?"

They'd barely spoken to each other since he'd told her that he was responsible for her father's death. Her grief was too raw, too close to the surface. Nearly every time he'd said anything to her, she'd started crying and walked out of the room.

"I'm guessing that's a no," Duncan said. "Has anyone figured out why her father was in the woods behind your house?"

Colin shrugged. "Gun powder residue tests were negative, so he wasn't the shooter. Other than that, I have no idea."

"Shooter? Singular? There was only one?"

"That's the consensus, although I haven't been able to tell Peyton." It was difficult to have that kind of conversation with someone who left the room every time he brought up the subject of her family. "There were only two sets of shoe prints—Mr. Sterling and someone else." Colin swatted at a horsefly out looking for an easy meal. It took off, searching for another target.

"Meaning Sterling junior was our shooter."

"Most likely." Colin checked his watch and frowned.

"Well at least the ambush makes more sense now," Duncan said. "From what I've heard, Brian blames you for everything from him being in prison to the marshals having the gall to keep searching for him. I can imagine his warped mind wanting revenge against you. What I can't understand is why he'd shoot at Peyton. I thought they were close."

"He didn't. The CSU guys confirmed the bullet trajectories, that all the shots from the woods were fired at the other side of the building, where I was. When she shot towards the woods, he was probably ducking for cover, assuming that I was the one shooting. I don't think he ever saw her. I was his only target."

Duncan tapped his boot, slowly nodding as if he was mulling everything over and putting the pieces together. As a criminal investigator, he often brainstormed with

Colin about things going on at either of their work-places. He was seldom wrong in his conclusions.

"Okay, how about this for a scenario?" Duncan asked. "Little brother and the other numbskulls split up, each of them trying to find their own way out of the mountains around the roadblocks. But Brian can't get out. He's frustrated, breaks into a parked car or some-one's cabin and steals a phone. Then he does what he's always done when things don't go his way—he calls Daddy to come rescue him. They both decide to enact a little vengeance on the man they feel is responsible for their woes and come up here to kill you."

"Pretty much what I came up with too. The part where Sterling senior wants to help his son kill me feels a bit off though. I have a hard time envisioning the fa-ther as a bloodthirsty criminal. But I haven't come up with a better explanation."

"Wait, you built this house long after the Sterlings moved away. And like most of us in law enforcement, you don't broadcast personal details like your home ad-dress on social media or anything. So how would Brian have known where you live?"

Colin started to cross his arms, then thought better of it when his ribs protested.

Duncan stared up at him, eyes widening. "Peyton told him, didn't she? I can't believe it. That little trai-tor. I should go arrest her right now. As a matter of fact, I think I will." He turned around and stalked to-ward his Jeep.

"Knock it off, Duncan. You can't arrest her for talk-ing to her father on the phone. She admitted she called to check on him after she arrived, and that she told him where she was staying. She had no reason to expect that her father would come here. And no one would have predicted that he and his son would decide to join forces and cause trouble."

Duncan turned around. "Cause trouble? They tried to murder you."

"Let it go." Colin checked his watch again. "And stop blaming Peyton. You know she could never purposely hurt anyone."

Duncan gestured down the road. "She's leaving you again. So much for not hurting anyone."

"Knock it off. I'm a big boy and can take care of myself. Besides, you need to cut her some slack. It's not like her life is all puppies and rainbows right now. Her mother died three months ago. Her brother is on the run. And her father was just killed."

Duncan shook his head. "I want to hate her for not sticking around. But you're right. I can't. Heck, we all grew up together. Mom still reminisces sometimes about the old days and talks about how she wishes things could have been different, that Peyton was still around." He spread his hands out in a helpless gesture. "I guess I'll be there to support her along with you at her father's funeral. When is it?"

"There isn't going to be one. When the coroner releases the body, it will be shipped to Memphis. Peyton said she's going to have a private memorial, 'private' meaning just her. Anything else seems inappropriate after everything that's happened. Her words, not mine. When she left here, she said she was going to the Sterling house to clean out the refrigerator and pack her things. Then she's heading to Memphis to close up her father's house and find a new place to live."

Duncan stared up at him, then slowly mounted the steps. "Then it's really over between you two? She's not coming back to Gatlinburg?"

Colin shook his head.

"Well, that makes this really awkward." He pulled a small box out of his suit jacket pocket and tossed it to Colin.

Colin held it up, then shot his brother a glance. "Condoms? You brought me a box of condoms?"

Duncan shrugged. "When two ex-lovers experience a life-or-death situation, one would expect that would bring them closer together. Thus, you know, the need for…protection. I thought I was doing you a favor. My timing, and apparently my instincts in that department, are a bit off."

"Apparently." Colin shook his head and shoved the box into his pants pocket for lack of anywhere else to put it.

"Guess I should go inside and take the whiskey now," Duncan said.

"Do and you die."

Duncan smiled and leaned against the opposite post. "Man, I can't believe she's actually leaving Gatlinburg. Again. What about her shop downtown?"

"She's giving it to her employees, along with some seed money to help them through until it's more profitable. She isn't sure what she's going to do but she wants a fresh start."

He arched a brow. "You sure I don't need to grab the whiskey?"

"I'm fine, Duncan. Knock it off." He wasn't fine of course. But he wasn't going to bare his soul to his brother out on his front porch. And this wasn't over, none of it, until he had Brian Sterling locked up again. Then he'd have to pick up the pieces and face whatever future he had—*somehow.*

"I imagine you'll be going back to work then, with Peyton out of the picture and the other marshals combing the mountains searching for our gang of fugitives."

"Nope. After the shooting, I have more incentive than ever to catch Brian. I haven't quit just yet."

"With all due respect for your great track record with locating fugitives, what makes you think you can do better than our law-enforcement brothers who are out looking for him right now?"

Colin glanced at his watch again. "I have something they don't."

"What would that be?"

"A GPS tracker on one of those fugitive's sister's SUV."

Duncan straightened. "I'm guessing that watch you keep checking isn't just a watch."

"Nope."

"Peyton didn't go to the Sterling homestead to clean out the refrigerator did she?"

"Didn't even slow down when she drove past the house. She's heading north toward town right now." Colin yanked his keys out of his pocket.

Duncan looked at him accusingly. "You thought she was innocent, that she wasn't helping her brother. So, why put a tracker on her car?"

"She *is* innocent. But she's also down to one family member and is an emotional wreck. I figure she's desperate enough to try to find him on her own before heading out of town. She'll think she's saving his life. If she does find him, I want to be there."

Duncan nodded his agreement. "To put Brian away."

"To protect Peyton. I programmed my phone number into her phone and told her to call me if she needs me. But I'm not sure she'll even realize that she's in danger if she manages to stumble across her brother. She wouldn't in a million years expect Brian to hurt her. I'm not nearly as trusting." He headed down the steps, forced to go slowly because of his ribs. "I'll call you later, let you know how it plays out."

"I strongly suggest that you let Landry or your fellow marshals handle this."

Colin looked back over his shoulder. "And tell them what? That I put a GPS tracker on my ex-girlfriend's car without her knowledge? That I'd like them to follow her just in case she meets up with her fugitive brother instead of, say, a new boyfriend? Does that sound a little stalker-ish to you?"

Duncan grinned. "When you put it that way, it's probably best that you don't mention it."

"Like I said, I'll call you later." He headed toward the garage.

Duncan hurried after him, pulling his phone out. "No way am I letting you do this alone. You need backup, just in case everything goes to hell again. And with the Sterlings, it usually does."

Colin entered a code on the keypad beside the garage and the door started up. He gestured toward the National Park Jeep. "That ugly monstrosity is in my way."

"You're just jealous that you don't have a green stripe down the side of your truck and a really cool arrowhead shaped emblem on your door."

"Yeah. That's it." Colin rolled his eyes.

"I'll move it. But don't even think about leaving without me." He raised his phone, then hesitated. "What am I going to tell my boss?"

Colin looked back. "Tell him the truth. You're going hunting."

Chapter Fifteen

Peyton patted the front and back pockets of her jeans again, mentally inventorying their contents as she approached the football field.

Quit acting so jumpy and nervous. He could be watching.

She forced herself to drop her hands to her sides and took several slow, deep breaths before sitting on the bottom row of the concrete bleachers. They were harder and less forgiving than she remembered. Then again, at eighteen, she probably wouldn't have noticed things like that. She'd been too busy noticing Colin McKenzie.

She glanced up and down the chain-link fence separating the bleachers from the field and the thick woods circling the area. The fence was in sad disrepair. Rusty top rails had popped out of their brackets in several places. In others, the rails were bent into deep Vs in the middle, as if the entire football team had used them as springboards to hop over the fence. Maybe they had. But as far as she could tell, the section directly in front of her was intact, which was why she'd chosen this particular spot to sit.

Come on, Brian. You have to be here. Because I don't know where else to look.

Since deciding at the last minute to go searching for him, she'd spent the entire day driving around town checking restaurants, stores, movie theaters. She'd even wasted an hour in Ripley's Aquarium, convinced he'd be there, somewhere. After all, that was where she and Brian would often go to de-stress when the fighting at home was too intense. But she hadn't even caught a glimpse of that familiar spikey blond hair or those silver-gray eyes so like her own. And her father's.

Oh, Daddy.

She breathed through the pain, ruthlessly locking away her emotions. She had to keep it together. Her family of four was down by half. If something happened to Brian, her family would no longer exist. She couldn't bear that, which was why she'd ended up here.

When she hadn't found her brother at any of his favorite spots, it had dawned on her that it was probably because he'd seen the police checking those same places. If he was on the run, and needed to disappear, then he'd try to hide where no one would ever expect him to go, somewhere he hated. And she couldn't think of any place he hated more than where he'd been picked on and bullied for four years—Gatlinburg–Pittman High School.

For her, this had been a happy place, a magical place. Because this was where she and Colin had fallen in love. They'd first met in the second grade, when she'd been taller than him and had ruthlessly chased him around the playground. After that, they'd been inseparable, a tomboy and her best friend who just happened to be a boy. They'd explored the woods, climbed tall trees that swayed in the wind and gotten a week's worth of extra chores as punishment when their parents found out.

They caught lightning bugs and he'd put a frog down her shirt. She'd retaliated by dumping ice water down his pants. She became a regular fixture in their household, spending more time with the McKenzies than she did at home, while Brian had remained on the fringes.

Her brother had never felt comfortable around the McKenzie family. He was quiet and reserved where they were loud and boisterous. He didn't like the outdoors, preferring to veg out playing video games all day. But he didn't mind that she hung out with Colin, as long as she spent time with him too. So they played video games together, even though she didn't like them. They'd ride their bikes down the mountain to the closest neighbor's house and bum a ride into town. And when he was struggling in middle school and had to repeat seventh grade, she'd started tutoring him, filling in the gap left by a mother who loved her son but didn't always know how to show it. She'd rather bake him cookies or try out her newest scented candles around the house than teach him to multiply fractions.

Then, everything changed. The summer before their freshman year in high school, fifteen-year-old Colin McKenzie transformed. Gone was the thin, lanky boy who sometimes tripped over his too-big feet. In his place was a confident young man who was growing into his frame. Muscles rippled in his arms and powerful thighs. Dark stubble lined his strong jaw where other guys his age still sported peach fuzz. His lean waist, narrow hips and broad shoulders had all the girls swooning on the first day of school, and that female attention never waned.

Not that he noticed.

Colin was only interested in one girl at school: Peyton. His newly deep, rich voice would send shivers up and down her spine, making her blush and making him grin. They'd shared many kisses behind these very bleachers, although their very first, magical kiss had been next to a waterfall on some beautiful land on the other side of the mountain from Colin's current home. Caught up in a bubble of happiness, she'd thought she'd died and gone to heaven.

Meanwhile, her brother had been floundering. And she hadn't even noticed.

She'd wanted to spend every free minute with her boy friend turned boyfriend. But Colin felt guilty taking her away from her brother so much. Especially since he was well aware of how rocky things were at the Sterling home. He insisted on including Brian in some of their outings, taking him with them to the occasional movie or dinner, even target practice. Brian might think of Colin as the devil now. But if it hadn't been for Colin's kindness in high school, Brian would have been even more lonely and miserable.

In his four years of high school, Brian had only made two friends. It would have been better if he hadn't. He'd managed to find the only kids in school more awkward and shy than himself. They looked up to him as their leader, which gave him confidence, but not in a good way. He'd acted out more than ever, leading the trio down a destructive path. Their petty thefts, graffiti and vandalism caused thousands of dollars in damage. And if Chief Landry was right, Brian had done far worse than that.

Did you really start fires as a kid, Brian? Are you the one who set the fire at the school dance, almost killing two people, hurting Colin, then blaming him for the choices you made?

If he had, she couldn't help but feel partly responsible.

"I'm so sorry, Brian," she whispered brokenly.

"For what?"

She jerked her head up.

Familiar gray eyes smiled back at her.

"Brian?"

She jumped up and threw herself against him. "I've been so scared. I'm so sorry. This is all my fault." She held on tight, moving her hands up and down his spine, hesitating when she felt the unmistakable outline of a gun shoved into the back pocket of his jeans. She squeezed her eyes shut against the tears that wanted to flow once again.

When he tried to step away, she hugged him fiercely, bumping hard against him and nearly knocking him over.

"Whoa, sis. Give a fella some air will ya?"

She let him go and straightened her blouse as she offered him a tight smile. "I've missed you so much. I'm so sorry."

He cocked his head. "What do you keep apologizing for?"

She gestured toward the bleachers, the field behind him, the school a hundred yards away. "This. All of it.

It's where the worst of your problems started. I wasn't there for you. I was too wrapped up in—"

"Colin?" He gave her a lopsided grin. "Three's a crowd, sis. Colin was one handsome dude. But he wasn't my type."

She blinked, then laughed, then hated herself for laughing because it seemed so insensitive, so wrong with everything that had happened.

He caught her hand and pulled her to the bleachers where they both sat down. "School was never my thing. And there wasn't anything you could have done to stop my downward spiral. Your superpowers didn't extend that far. But you could bake an amazing chocolate chip cookie."

She tried to smile. But her heart wasn't in it. "I wish I could do it all over again. Like at the last school dance. The barn."

"Don't." His jaw tightened and he braced his forearms on his thighs, hands clasped together. "I don't want to talk about that."

"But we went there together. It was supposed to be a party and I promised I'd get some of my friends to dance with you. Colin was on a trip out of town with his family. I didn't expect him to get home early and come looking for me. But when he did, I should have told him no, that I was there with you."

"Trust me, sis. It wouldn't have changed a thing if you had."

She frowned. "But if we'd stayed together, or if I'd encouraged you to stay with Mom when she was chaperoning—"

He snorted. "Yeah. Mom the chaperone, keeping everyone safe. Wasn't that a joke."

"What do you mean?"

He gave her a sideways glance, shrugged. "She was a space cadet. Not tuned in to things going on around her. She'd rather roast those stupid s'mores in the fireplace than spend quality time with her kids." He shook his head. "How many s'mores can one person eat? And who uses their fireplace in the summer? Didn't you think she was weird?"

"I prefer to think of her as eccentric. But she's gone now. I don't see the point in disparaging her."

"To each his own."

"I thought you adored Mom. You were her favorite."

He scrubbed his hands against his jeans. Funny that she'd never noticed before that he had the same habit she did.

"Mom liked me because we liked the same things. She saw herself in me and didn't feel as weird, you know?"

She didn't know, but she nodded anyway.

"Now Dad, he and I had *nothing* in common. He couldn't stand me. But you were *his* favorite. I guess it evened out."

He sounded so cold speaking about their father. But she believed it was mostly bluster, a defense mechanism by a boy who'd always loved his dad, even if his dad seemed incapable of returning that love. The police had been able to keep the shooting out of the news so far, but that wouldn't last forever. She should tell him, now, but she wasn't ready.

She looked toward the trees on the far side of the

field, back over her shoulder. "What happened to the guys you escaped with? Should I be worried that they're watching me from the woods?"

"I'm not going to let anything happen to you, sis. You were always there for me growing up. I owe you my protection, even if you are consorting with the enemy." He motioned toward the parking lot. "Where's your boyfriend hiding?"

Her stomach jumped. "Boyfriend? Hiding?"

"Tell the truth. Are you bait? He's hiding somewhere hoping to catch me?"

Her pulse leaped in her throat; his teasing tone had an underlying bitterness that sent a chill down her spine. "I'm all alone, Brian. He doesn't know I'm here."

His brows raised. "Snuck out, did you? Huh. Could it be you miss dear old bro after all? You just wanted to see me?"

Standing, she crossed her arms and moved to the fence, hoping he'd follow. "I did miss you, do miss you. I'm worried about you."

He pushed to his feet and joined her. "You always did worry about me." His smile seemed genuine, like the old Brian she'd once known. "But that's not your job anymore. It's time for me to take care of me, wrap up a few loose ends."

"L-loose ends?"

"Colin McKenzie, for one."

The bottom dropped out of her stomach. "But... I don't want you to do anything to Colin."

"Yeah, I know." He clucked his tongue. "But a guy's got to do what a guy's got to do. I'll protect you. You have my word on that. But I'm afraid you're going to have to live with at least one more tragic loss in your near future." He leaned against the top rail. It squeaked in protest.

His callous confession that he planned to hurt Colin had her wanting to throw up. And more committed than ever to her plan. She had to stop him, stop whatever he was planning. But she also wanted more information. She had so many questions, so many things she didn't understand. "Why do you hate him so much?"

His grin faded. "He testified against me. Fifteen years, Peyton. He and his fellow Mighty McKenzies put pressure on the judge and got me fifteen years."

"There were other kids roaming the property that night, instead of staying inside the dance hall like we were supposed to. Colin wasn't the only one who testified that they saw you outside the barn, running away right before the fire. How do you explain that?"

"Explain it?" He leaned toward her, his mood changing lightning fast, anger blazing in his quicksilver eyes. "Fine. Truth. I *was* in that barn that night."

"Oh, Brian."

"But I didn't start the fire! Sure, I saw that stupid gas can. Some idiot had knocked it over, spilling gas all over a hay bale. I was worried someone would do something stupid, like sneak out of the dance and into the barn to smoke a couple of cigarettes without realizing the fumes could light the place up like a roman candle." He jabbed his thumb toward his chest. "I was being the responsible one. I was trying to *prevent* a fire. I ran the can outside, fully intending to warn people away from the place. When I came back, it was already going up in flames." He shook his head, his lips curling in a sneer.

"And your *precious Colin* gets all the credit for being the good guy, for saving those stupid fools who never should have gone in there in the first place. There. Is that enough truth for you?"

"But Brian, if that's what happened, it changes everything. It explains why people said they saw you with a gas can. Did you tell your lawyer?"

He laughed, but didn't sound amused. "Dear old Mom and Dad told me not to."

She pressed her hand to her throat. "What are you saying? That doesn't make sense."

"Yeah, well, in hindsight, not being a green nineteen-year-old kid anymore, I agree with you. But they insisted that no one would believe me, that I'd be admitting I was at the scene of the crime. They said my best shot at an acquittal was for my lawyer to discredit the witnesses. There wasn't any forensic evidence that proved I started a fire. Showing reasonable doubt would be a slam dunk." He wrapped his fingers around the pole, his knuckles turning white. "Not such a slam dunk after all, was it? And here we are, folks. Once again Brian goes down in flames for something he didn't do. I didn't plan the stupid jailbreak. And I didn't shoot that cop. But I'll still get the death penalty. Felony murder. Guilt by association. Which is why I need to get out of here before someone else figures out where I am."

"No, wait."

He frowned. "What?"

She had to keep him distracted, put her plan into motion. It was time to tell him about their father. "A couple of nights ago, there was a shooting, at Colin's house—"

He looked away. "Yeah. Heard about that."

"Then you know? About dad? He was…he was killed in the woods that night. Colin… Colin shot him while returning gunfire."

"Dear old dad tried to get payback for what your boyfriend did to me. Huh. Guess the old man did something good for his son for once in his life."

"Oh, Brian. How can you be so callous about our own father?"

He leaned against the fence, the top bar wobbling beneath his weight. "You're so naive, even now, aren't you? Daddy cared about Daddy—and the Sterling name. That's all he cared about. Why do you think he bought my way out of trouble all the time? It sure wasn't because he cared about me. He cared about how it would look. That's why I called him, told him to meet me."

"You called him? And he met with you at Colin's place? You were there?" Her voice broke on the last word.

Something flashed in his eyes. Confusion? Pain? Regret? Then he let out a deep breath. "I told him if he brought me enough money, I'd disappear. For good. He'd never have to worry about me dragging his precious name through the gutter again. But when he showed up, he didn't bring money. He brought a stupid lecture. The son of a gun must have finally developed a conscience after all."

She was starting to go numb inside, no longer processing the revelations he was making. Instead, she kept her focus on her plan. She slid her hand into her back pocket, then clasped both hands together and put them on top of the railing next to his. When he didn't look down, she moved her left hand oh so carefully, then put her right hand just slightly on top of his and leaned forward to cover what she was doing, looking down at the ground as if she'd seen something.

He frowned and leaned over the rail. "What are you looking at?"

One more slight adjustment. *Click. Click.*

She jumped back, stumbling and catching herself against the fence a few yards away. The whole thing wobbled, seeming much more unstable than she'd realized.

He frowned in confusion, then started toward her. He jerked up short, catching himself against the fence. "What the—" He looked down, confusion turning to fury when he saw the handcuff circling his wrist, the other end circling the top pole.

"I'm so sorry," she told him. "But I can't let you go. You have to stay and face what you've done."

He rattled the cuffs, his face turning red. "You conniving little…" He yanked his arm, straining against the railing. "Take them off. Now."

She backed up several more feet, his anger like a palpable force, thickening the air between them. "I took them from Colin's house. I don't have a key." She pulled her phone out of her front pocket.

His eyes narrowed. "Don't."

"I have to." She punched her favorites folder.

He cursed at her, saying things that pierced her heart like shards of glass.

Whirling to face the top rail, he grabbed it with both hands and pulled, his biceps bulging beneath the strain. The bar made a metallic screeching sound, then popped. The chain link fencing sagged away, leaving the top rail leaning toward the left, but still attached to both poles. Barely.

Peyton stared in horror as he slid the cuff along the rail toward the pole on the left. Using his free hand, he yanked and tugged on the bar some more. The bracket holding the pole creaked.

"Brian, stop. Please. I'm trying to help you." Her hands shook so hard she was having trouble pressing the preprogrammed number on her phone.

"Turns out you're as fake as everyone else," he sneered. "All you care about is dear old Colin." He spat the name at her like acid.

He moved back as far as his arm would allow, then slammed his shoe against the rail. It bent, but held. He moved back again, raised his foot.

Peyton desperately pushed the number and hit Send.

Brian slammed his shoe against the railing a second time. A piece of metal flew off the bracket, landing on the concrete with a metallic clang. The railing fell, jerking Brian to the ground as the handcuff caught on what was left of the broken bracket.

"US Marshal. Put your hands in the air, both of you!"

Peyton froze at the sound of Colin's voice behind her and slowly did as he'd said, her phone still clutched in her right hand.

Brian tugged and pulled at the cuffs.

"Don't move, Brian!" Colin yelled.

Brian jerked the cuffs loose from the broken bracket, but remained crouched on the ground with Peyton between him and Colin. He glanced up at her, one handcuff still attached to his wrist, the other dangling from the small chain. She'd never seen such a look of pure hate before.

He grabbed for his back pocket, then whirled around, looking at the ground, then up and down the perimeter of fence.

A bone deep cold crept through Peyton's body as she watched her brother searching for his gun so he could kill Colin, or her. Or both.

"Peyton," Colin yelled, his shoes thumping against the ground as he ran toward her. "Get down."

Brian cursed viciously and took off running.

Peyton tried to duck. She tried to obey his shouted command. But she couldn't move. Was this what it felt like to die? To have every organ in her body shut down at the same time? To have her heart shatter in her chest?

"Peyton!" Colin yelled again.

Brian disappeared behind the bleachers.

Colin stopped beside her, his gun pointed up toward the sky.

Duncan sprinted past them. She hadn't even realized he was there. Pistol in hand, he stopped at the end of the bleachers, peered around the concrete supports then disappeared.

Colin stared at her, his brows drawn down as he holstered his gun. "Why didn't you move out of the way? He could have shot you and there wasn't a thing I could do about it."

She shook her head. "He couldn't shoot me."

His jaw tightened. "After all he's done, how can you think he wouldn't—"

"I didn't say he *wouldn't*. I said he *couldn't*." She lifted the back of her shirt and pulled the pistol out of the waistband of her jeans and carefully handed it to him.

"He had that in his back pocket when he first got here," she explained, as Colin checked the loading before shoving the pistol in his own back pocket. "I took it when I hugged him. He didn't realize it until after I'd handcuffed him to the fence and he broke free. Actually, I'm still not sure he realized I took it. Maybe he thought he dropped it."

His face went pale. "You took a loaded gun from your brother? And handcuffed him to the fence?" He glanced behind her. "The fence that's falling down?"

"Yeah, well. I thought this section was solid enough to hold him. I was wrong." She shrugged and tried to smile. Then burst into tears and covered her face.

Colin's hands were shaking when he pulled her against his chest. His sharp intake of breath had her trying to push out of his arms.

"Your bruises. I don't want to hurt—"

"Forget the bruises. Come here, sweetheart."

The endearment, the first time he'd called her that in over ten years, had her throwing herself into his arms and soaking his shirt with her tears.

"Shh, it's okay. Everything's going to be okay." He rubbed her back and rested his cheek on the top of her head.

She clung to him, then gasped and scrambled out of his arms again. "Duncan. He needs backup. What if—"

"We came with backup. As soon as I realized you were going here, surrounded by woods that I couldn't secure, I called Landry and the marshals. Half a dozen of them are out there right now looking for Brian. More are on the way. Don't worry about Duncan. He'll be okay."

She swallowed and wiped her tears. "I don't understand. How could you get help so fast? I only just now called you."

He frowned and pulled his phone out. "So you did. It's on vibrate mode. I was too busy sneaking up behind you and Brian to notice it."

She stiffened. "Sneaking up behind me and Brian? Both of us? You, what? Thought I went over to the dark side and was helping my fugitive brother?"

"You know better than that."

She fisted her hands beside her. "Do I? You said you called the others once you realized where I was going. You were following me, admit it."

He shoved his phone into his pocket. "You told me you were going home to pack. You didn't even stop at your house and continued down the mountain."

She stared at him, trying to make sense of what he was saying. "How would you know that? What did you do, put some kind of tracking device on my car?"

He stared at her but didn't say anything.

"That was sarcasm," she told him. "This is the part where you say, no, of course I didn't put a freaking GPS tracker on your car." When he didn't say anything, her mouth dropped open. "You did! After everything we've been through, after I risked my life for you during the shooting, you still don't trust me."

"It's not about trusting you. It's about not trusting your brother, and understanding that a sister of course is going to try to help him. If you somehow figured out where he was, I wanted to make sure you were safe. I was going to—"

Duncan jogged back from behind the bleachers, breathing hard. He slowed to a stop a few yards away, glancing uncertainly back and forth between them. "What did I miss?"

Peyton narrowed her eyes. "Did you know that Colin had a tracking device on my car?"

He blinked. "I, uh—"

"Wait, you came here together didn't you? Of course you knew he was tracking me. Son of a—"

"Duncan, was there something you were going to tell me?" Colin asked, sounding exasperated.

Duncan gave Peyton an apologetic look before answering. "The marshals took over the chase. He's heading west through the woods. They've called for air support."

"Well," Peyton said. "Sounds like you boys have everything under control. Great. That's just great. Now, if you'll excuse me, I have to return to Memphis to settle my father's affairs."

Colin stepped toward her. "We need to talk."

"You put a *tracker* on my *car*."

"You lied about where you were going."

"You put the tracker on my car *before* I lied to you. And I didn't lie! I changed my mind!"

"Seriously? You changed your mind? That's your explanation?"

"My explanation is that I was trying to protect you. I decided at the last minute to try to find my brother before I left, to see if I could bring a peaceful conclusion to this ever-loving mess. And as you already know, I called you to tell you he was here."

His face reddened. "You were protecting me? You offered yourself up as bait to an arsonist!"

"Arsonist according to you."

"According to a jury. Did you forget that part? And the fifteen-year sentence?"

She crossed her arms.

He swore. "I can't believe you purposely put yourself in danger, again. Did you learn nothing the other night when you were nearly killed?"

She gasped, then whirled around and marched toward her car.

"Peyton, come back here."

She stopped, and looked over her shoulder. "Are you arresting me, Marshal McKenzie?"

His eyes narrowed. "You know damn well I'm not, *Miss Sterling*. But you need to give a formal statement about what happened here. And you and I need to talk."

"You and I have *nothing* to talk about. I'll phone my statement in to Chief Landry."

"Peyton—"

She stalked to her car and slammed the door, twice, just to make herself feel better. Then she gunned the engine and peeled out of the parking lot, mentally daring the uniformed cops who were just turning in to try to give her a ticket.

She'd only made it about five miles down the road before her flood of tears forced her to pull over. Hands shaking, she cut the engine and drew deep, even breaths, desperately trying to get a handle on her grief and pain. The way she'd treated Colin was unconscionable. Even while she was lashing out at him, she'd known it was wrong. That the hateful emotions spilling out of her weren't meant for him.

They were meant for Brian.

And her mom, for doting on her son one moment and ignoring him the next.

Her father, for the selfishness that had him so angry over being ignored by his obsessed-with-baking wife that he'd ignored the little boy who desperately needed his affection.

But mostly, she was to blame. Forever taking for granted the one truly good, honorable, decent person in her life. When had she ever been there for Colin when he'd needed her? And yet, every time life was imploding on her, he'd been there.

Movement in her rearview mirror had her looking up to see a familiar dark blue pickup truck pull onto the shoulder behind her. Colin. He looked in his mirrors before popping open his door and jumping down.

Peyton choked on a sob, then threw her door open and ran to him. But she stumbled to a halt a few feet away when she remembered his bruised chest. "Colin, I'm so sorry. What I said was—"

He stepped forward and pulled her against him, hugging her tight.

She clutched the back of his shirt. "Your bruises. You shouldn't—"

"Stop worrying about me. All right?" He gently rubbed his hand up and down her back as he held her against him.

He seemed content to stand there on the side of the road, holding her without any regard for the occasional car that drove by. She never wanted to let him go. Which was why she forced herself to drop her hands and step back.

She wrapped her arms around her middle and leaned against her SUV. "I can't believe you came to check on me after how horribly I acted back there."

"I wasn't exactly a saint myself at the school." His mouth crooked up in amusement. "And, actually, I came for this." He leaned past her and reached under the bumper, then straightened, holding up a metal disc with a blinking red light. "Tracker," he explained, before shoving it in his pants pocket. "I figured you'd think about it eventually, then realize it was still there and get even more upset."

He looked over the top of her head, toward the woods on either side of the highway, ever the alert marshal, always aware of his surroundings. When he looked down at her again, his eyes had darkened with concern, and something else.

"Peyton, I owe you a huge apology. I never should have—"

She pressed her hand against his mouth and shook her head. "Don't. It's okay. I understand why you did it. I destroyed your trust years ago. Then I compounded it by helping a convicted felon escape my house when you could have taken him into custody, right then and there." She feathered her fingers gently down the front of his shirt, careful not to press against his ribs. "You wouldn't have gotten shot. My daddy…my father would still be alive. And you wouldn't have put your life on the line yet again to save me from my own brother at the high school."

He cupped her face, forcing her to meet his gaze. "Let's stop with the self-recriminations and just agree that these are extraordinary circumstances and we're both imperfect. We've both made mistakes. We both have regrets." He searched her gaze. "What I need to know is that you're going to be okay. Are you sure you want to do this? Drive back to Memphis right now, alone? I could—"

She turned her head and kissed his palm before gently tugging his hands down. "I'm okay. Or, I will be. Really. Just seeing you again has made all the difference." She smiled up at him. "I need to do this, settle things, say goodbye to my father. Hopefully all of this—" she motioned in the air "—will be over soon, one way or the other. And then, maybe we can talk, like we should have years ago, and see where things end up."

He frowned. "Peyton—"

"You need to be extra careful. Brian's planning something. He blames you for everything, wants revenge."

"No surprise there."

"I mean it, Colin. Please, watch your back."

"I will. Promise." He smiled reassuringly.

She shoved her hair out of her face. "There are other things I need to tell you, for the investigation, things Brian said. A lot of it doesn't make sense. It's all so confusing. But I can't… I can't talk about it just yet. I'll call you, answer your questions over the phone. Maybe in a few hours, on the long drive to Memphis. Is that okay?"

"Of course. But you don't have to leave. You can stay—"

"Don't. I'm barely keeping myself together. There is

so much grief and pain for me back here. So much." A sob escaped, but she breathed through it, held her grief in check. "In spite of what you may think, given our history, walking away from you isn't easy to do. And I don't…" She shook her head. "I need some time. I need to think." She stood on her tiptoes and kissed his cheek. "Take care of yourself, Colin McKenzie."

COLIN BRACED HIS hands behind him on the hood of his truck, using every ounce of his willpower to keep from chasing after Peyton as she drove away for the second time that day. He ached to take her in his arms, beg her not to leave. But it wouldn't be fair to her. She wanted time to think, whatever that meant. And he had to give it to her. But that didn't make it easy. As the sun began to set, he wondered if it was also setting on the last remaining hopes that the two of them could ever escape the echoes of their past.

His phone buzzed in his pocket. When he saw who was calling, he climbed in his truck and shut the door. "Hey Duncan. Tell me you found him. I'm ready for this to be over."

"Did you find *her*?"

He'd just started the engine, but hesitated at the urgency in his brother's voice. "I did. We talked. She's on her way to Memphis now. Why?"

"She was alone? No one could have been hiding in her car?"

He fisted his hand on the steering wheel, disappointment slamming through him at his brother's question. "You're telling me Brian got away? Don't worry about Peyton. I was standing by her back window while we were talking. No one could have hidden inside. I can't believe he escaped again. That guy is slipperier than a water moccasin and twice as deadly."

"You need to get back here, to the high school."

Duncan's voice was hoarse. Colin couldn't remember the last time he'd sounded so shaken.

"What's going on?"

"The police are pretty sure they found the other three escapees, a mile east of the school in a heavily wooded area."

"*Pretty* sure? What does that mean?" Colin checked his mirrors, then turned around in the middle of the highway and headed toward the school.

"They were tied to the base of an oak tree. Someone had poured some kind of accelerant on them and lit them on fire. They're unrecognizable. The only reason the cops think it's them is because someone carved initials into the tree facing them—DP, VS, TK—Damon Patterson, Vincent Snyder, Tyler King." He let out a shuddering breath. "Colin, the police found them because they heard their screams."

"For the love of…" Colin let out a shaky breath of his own, his stomach roiling at the images his brother's words conjured in his mind. He flexed his hand on the steering wheel, the spiderweb of burn scars standing out in stark relief against his tan. "Brian's escalated from setting buildings on fire without worrying whether someone might be inside to deliberately setting *people* on fire. Honestly, I never imagined he was capable of something that heinous. Kind of makes me glad Peyton left. I don't even want her in the same state as her psychotic sibling."

"Psychotic sounds about right, someone out of touch with the normal world, for sure. But it gets worse. Remember I told you that after I chased Brian into the woods behind the bleachers, the marshals we'd called were already out there and took over the pursuit?"

"Yeah, go on."

"They couldn't fire any shots at him because some residences were close by. They lost him when he jumped into a vehicle he'd left strategically parked for a quick getaway—a stolen car, obviously. That car was a mile west of the school, *two miles* from where they found the bodies."

Colin tightened his grip on the steering wheel. "You said they were still screaming when they were found?"

"Yes. Any idea how long it would take someone's lungs to incinerate and for them to lose the ability to scream in a situation like that?"

"I'm guessing not long. Is the medical examiner on the way?"

"ETA five minutes."

"I'll be there in two."

Chapter Sixteen

Peyton clutched the cell phone in her hand as she stared at the papers and photo albums covering the top of her father's dining room table. She had to make the call. She *would* make the call. But not yet. She needed a few more minutes alone with the horror that her life had become before she shared this latest batch of awful family secrets. Especially since the person she was going to share them with was the one person whose opinion of her and her family mattered—Colin.

Her hand shook as she straightened one of the stacks of medical bills before lowering herself to perch on an olive-green cushioned chair. In the week since her father's memorial service, she'd sorted through all of his belongings, setting aside items to donate to charity and others to be thrown out. And this, a handful of photo albums and several stacks of bills and paperwork, had painted a picture she'd never imagined she would see, even in her worst nightmares.

When she'd helped her father sort through her mother's things months earlier, he'd insisted on being the one to go up in the attic to bring down the boxes. Now she knew why. He hadn't wanted her to see these *particular* boxes. Because they contained bills and letters and photographs that laid bare a family history that would shred what little was left of the one thing that her father treasured above all else—the Sterling reputation.

Her hand started to ache and she realized she was gripping the phone too tightly. She set the phone down on the edge of the table, then slowly flipped through an old photo album that documented her mother's life from the time she was a child through the first years of her marriage to Peyton's father. The cardboard backing was brittle, the time-yellowed protective plastic covers crinkling each time she turned a page.

The baby pictures had been shocking enough, because Peyton and Brian had been told that there weren't any baby pictures of their mother, that she'd been an orphan, raised in foster care, and didn't have any knowledge of her birth family. Judging by the smiling faces of the many relatives surrounding baby Molly, that had been a lie.

Later pictures showed her mother with the same people, who were taking the happy toddler to a fair to ride ponies, pushing her on a swing at the park. She grew up on the pages in front of Peyton, learning to ride a bike, starting elementary school, holding up her fifth-grade report card while holding her nose, as if laughing at the bad grades she'd made. The transition from happy smiling baby to morose teenager in the second half of the album was startling to see. It reminded her so much of Brian that her heart ached.

The next-to-last page showed a two-story brick house with acres of rolling green hills behind it. No mountains, so it wasn't near Gatlinburg. Dozens of smiling, well-dressed people Peyton recognized from throughout the album—her mother's family—posed in front of the house. And in the middle, holding hands and smiling at the camera, was a blond woman with blue eyes in a bridal gown beside a thin man with silver-gray eyes in a business suit. Her mother and father, looking impossibly young and happier than she'd ever seen them. Obviously her mother hadn't aged out of the foster system with no relatives. Her entire history had been one big lie. And all Peyton had to do was turn the final page to discover why her parents had lied, why they didn't want anyone to know about her mother's real past.

Faded newsprint preserved behind plastic showed the article's title in big, bold letters.

Sorority House Fire Kills Three.

Below the headline was a group of six young sorority sisters from the house, clinging to each other in their nightgowns, tears running down their soot-streaked faces. Except one. Molly Andrews. She wasn't crying. She was smiling for the camera as the flames eerily reflected in her eyes and firemen struggled to bring the fire under control.

The story below the photograph was only two short paragraphs. Not much to tell in the early stages of the investigation. It simply said that the women pictured were the lucky survivors of the early morning house fire and that it was believed to have started in the kitchen. Molly Andrews of Chattanooga, Tennessee, mentioned that Sarah Engler—one of the girls who'd perished— had a habit of leaving the gas stove turned on. Molly openly wondered whether a dish towel may have been too close to the stove and caught on fire. Molly Andrews was a slightly younger version of the woman in the wedding picture in this same album. But there was no question that she was Peyton's mom, even though her mother's maiden name was supposed to be Tate and she was from Nashville, not Chattanooga.

Or so Brian and Peyton had been told. Yet another lie in a growing list of them.

She set the album aside and slid one of the stacks of bills toward herself. This was a stack that her father had also kept hidden in a box in the attic, and added even more details to her mother's story that she'd never known. The therapist her mother had been seeing for years wasn't a marriage counselor after all. He was a doctor who specialized in the treatment of addictive disorders, rage issues and impulse control problems. Exactly the kind of doctor who'd treated Brian when he'd gotten in trouble with the law and was forced to go to therapy.

But those weren't the only doctors her mother had been seeing.

A month before the car accident, she'd been diagnosed with stage four metastatic cancer, with tumors in her liver and her brain. Based on the doctor's notes in one of the folders that Peyton had found, her parents had decided not to take extraordinary measures. No chemotherapy. No radiation. Just pills to help control her mother's pain.

Oh, Mom. Why didn't you or Dad tell me? I would have been there for both of you. That's what families do.

Except, apparently, hers.

Once again, her parents had chosen to keep secrets

from their children. But even that wasn't the final bomb-shell that had exploded in Peyton's life these past few days. There was one more box in the attic. A box of old-fashioned handwritten letters, possibly because the sender had given up on getting any replies to their electronic messages. All of the letters were neatly folded in their original envelopes. And all of them had been sent during that first year after Brian's arrest for the barn fire.

Half of them had been mailed to the Sterling home in Gatlinburg and the post office had forwarded them. The sender must have figured out their new address in Memphis after that, because the rest of them had been mailed directly here. But her father, claiming he wanted to protect the family from ugly, harassing letters people often sent about Brian as his trial loomed, had all of the family's mail forwarded to a post office box. Peyton had never seen any of these letters before.

Letters sent to *her*. By Colin McKenzie.

She picked up the phone again. It was time to face the past, to shine the light of truth on her family's secrets. She couldn't put the shame off any longer. Because somewhere out there were three families who'd lost their beloved daughters or sisters in a sorority house fire that Peyton's internet search had discovered was ruled accidental. Peyton didn't believe that for a second. And those families deserved to know the truth.

Colin answered on the first ring. "Peyton? Is everything okay?"

She smiled. His first words were concern about her. Why couldn't everyone be that decent, that wonderful? The world would be such a better place.

"Hi, Colin. No, unfortunately, everything is not okay. I need to see you. We need to talk. In person."

"Where are you? I'll get there as fast as I can."

"Still in Memphis, my dad's house. I'll come to you. The drive will help clear my mind. But obviously it's going to be late when I get there. Is that okay? Have you gone back to work yet? I don't want you showing up at the office unable to keep your eyes open because of me. I could stay at my house—"

"No. Don't. I asked Chief Landry to post someone on your property to keep an eye on things while you were gone. It would be better if you come here."

So he could keep her safe, no doubt. From her own brother. A tear slid down her cheek. She hadn't realized that she had any tears left. "Okay. Thanks. I'll go directly to your place."

"The curiosity and worry is going to eat me alive during your six-hour drive. Can you at least give me a hint what this is about? Maybe just the headlines?"

The picture of the sorority fire newspaper clipping flashed in her mind. "Headlines," she whispered brokenly. "Funny you would say that."

"Peyton?"

"Okay. The headlines. I know I've been a broken record over the years, claiming my brother didn't start the barn fire. Over the past few weeks, I'd pretty much decided I was wrong, that you and everyone else are right, in spite of what he said at the school, that I told you about over the phone on my drive here. But part of what he told me might be true. I've got a new theory about who started that fire. I believe this person probably started a lot of fires over the years, one in particular with deadly consequences."

He hesitated. "Do you have a name?"

"Molly Andrews of Chattanooga, also known as Molly Tate, aka Molly Sterling. My mother."

Chapter Seventeen

Colin set the photo album on top of the piles of papers that Peyton had spread out on his coffee table. She sat across from him on the other couch, her hands clasped together so hard that her knuckles had gone white. He waved to the newspaper clipping with its headline about the sorority house fire.

"I understand why that newspaper article would alarm you, especially considering everything that you've discovered and Brian's conviction. But while it raises suspicions, none of it is evidence of arson."

She motioned toward the album. "I didn't think cops—or marshals—believed in coincidences. That sorority fire is an awfully big one."

"Because your mom survived a fire as a young woman and her son was later convicted of arson?"

She nodded.

"Honestly, it doesn't raise any eyebrows for me, given that your mom doesn't have a criminal record. After our earlier phone call, I checked. Under all three names. The fire at her college is the only mention of her that I could find in any law-enforcement databases."

"Okay, well, how about the therapist she was seeing? Her and Dad lied about it, pretended it was marriage counseling." She spread out some of the papers, then extracted the stack of bills from the doctor and held them up. "I looked this guy up online. He's testified as an expert in two arson cases." She tossed the bills back onto the coffee table. "And there are other things—my mom's fascination with candles. She was always buying new scents. We always had lit candles in our house. And the fireplace. Even in the summer she'd have a fire going. Looking back, that seems like an unhealthy fascination with fire to me. And don't you dare start talking about how much you loved the s'mores she used to cook in the fireplace. You have to admit it's odd."

"Okay. I won't mention that I absolutely loved coming over to your house for s'mores in the summer."

She frowned.

"Or that my mom loves candles, too."

"Colin—"

"And that the vanilla-scented candles your mom was so fond of have a special place in my childhood memories. Your house always smelled great."

She spread her hands out. "Why are you fighting me on this?"

"I'm not fighting you. I'm saying that if you look at each thing by itself, it loses the sinister significance that you're attaching to it. If you want me to investigate your mom, I absolutely will. But are you sure you want that? As soon as anyone hears even a whiff of this, rumors will start running rampant. You won't be able to put that cat back in the bag. Your mother's reputation will be forever tarnished."

Rubbing her hands against her jeans, she seemed to consider everything, then nodded. "Yes. I want you to start an investigation on her. I understand the risks. But it's the right thing to do."

"Because you believe it could prove that Brian didn't start the barn fire?"

"No. I mean, it might. But that's not why I want you to look into this. It no longer matters whether he was innocent back then. He's changed. Maybe prison changed him or he fooled me all along and I'm only now seeing it. I'm telling you, Colin. He scared me at the high school. And his hate for you knows no bounds. He tried to kill you once already, and he'll try again if he's not caught. As far as I'm concerned, he needs to go back to prison for a very long time to keep everyone else safe. So, no, none of this is for him. It's for the families of those sorority girls. If that sorority fire wasn't an accident, if my mom was to blame, they deserve to know."

He shook his head in wonder. "I hope you can let go of all the guilt you carry around someday. Because you have a really good heart. You're a good person, Peyton. The very best."

She blinked several times, then pressed her fingers against her eyes. "You'd better stop. You're going to get me crying again. And I am so sick of crying." She dropped her hands and offered him a watery smile. "So you'll do it? You'll investigate?"

"I will. I'll talk to my boss, see if he'll make it official. That will make it easier to get the information I'll need, lend the investigation more authority with witnesses. Arson that causes deaths comes under federal purview. I should be able to take it on."

"Thank you. I really appreciate it."

"You bet. But there's one more thing I want to put out there, just in case it changes your mind. Statistics."

"Statistics?"

"On arson. Most arson is done for profit. With the barn fire, there was no insurance. There weren't any highway projects or real estate developments coming through that wanted the property and were trying to intimidate an owner who refused to sell. No matter who set the fire, profit wasn't the motive."

"Agreed. That makes sense."

"Another primary motive is to hide another crime, like to cover up a murder. Fire destroys evidence. In this case, no one was killed—"

"Thanks to you."

He shrugged. "The kids I pulled out of there were just that, high school kids like you and me. They snuck in for a make-out session. They didn't have any enemies that the investigation could find. So, again, covering up a crime doesn't seem like the reason behind the fire either. Not from any evidence that I've seen. That pretty much leaves us the psychological reasons, which is what was presented at Brian's trial. The prosecution argued that he was a firebug, that starting fires for him was a compulsion, an impulse control problem."

"Impulse control is one of the specialties of the doctor who treated my mom."

"That's also a specialty of the doctor who treated Brian when your dad made a deal to keep him from being charged as a juvenile."

"The fires Chief Landry mentioned?"

He nodded.

She sat back, rubbing her arms as if to ward off a chill. "I knew he'd gotten in trouble, of course. But I never knew about those fires, and just how much trouble, until the chief mentioned it. I thought all this time that Brian was getting help for his anger issues, learning to channel his energy in more constructive ways. I had no idea it was this bad. Chalk that up to one more lie my parents told me."

"I imagine they were trying to protect you. You were young, with your whole life ahead of you. Maybe they wanted you to be happy and not be dragged down by all the worry they were going through."

"Maybe. It's dragging me down now, that's for sure."

"Then I'll get right to the point. Thrill-seekers, pyromaniacs, are extremely rare in the world of arson. Which makes having two in one family more unlikely than likely. But it's the last statistic that's the most telling. Over ninety percent of arsonists are white males. The episodes are often driven by anger. And intelligence is generally lower than your average person. Not always, but the majority of the time. It seems to have to do with their ability to reason and think through the effects of their crimes. The lower intelligence contributes to their lack of impulse control. Be honest. Does that sound like your mother or your brother?"

She was quiet for a moment, then nodded. "Mom was more on an even keel, really calm—unless she was fighting with Dad. Then again, he was the one doing most of the yelling. Yeah, it sounds like Brian."

He rested his forearms on his thighs and clasped his hands together. "It's getting pretty late. I know you must be tired. Do you want to stop?"

She stifled a yawn, then smiled. "That was your fault, for reminding me how tired I am. But, no. If there's more that you can tell me, I want to hear it. If you can prove to me that my mom's innocent, I'll sleep a lot better tonight."

"I don't know that I can definitely prove she's innocent. But we can talk about the fire. We never have before. You sure you want me to go on?"

"I'm sure. But—" she motioned toward his hands "—I don't know that it's fair to ask you to do that after everything you suffered because of that night."

"It was a long time ago. I'm more than willing to discuss what happened in light of your questions about your mom. The night of the barn fire, she was a chaperone right? In the dance hall?"

"Yes. I think there were seven or eight chaperones. The dance hall was huge. Half the senior class was there. No one was supposed to leave the building, but of course a lot of people snuck out here and there. The setting was gorgeous, lots of paths through the woods, waterfalls and party lights throughout, strung on pergolas and buildings. A great place for couples."

He smiled at the memory. "It was beautiful. So were you. I seem to remember arriving late, getting a couple of dances, then sneaking you outside to steal some kisses by a waterfall."

She shook her head, but a smile played about her lips. "You were always stealing kisses by waterfalls. One of our favorite waterfalls was on the other side of the mountain from this place. I can't remember a more beautiful view in all of the Smokies."

Her smile turned sad and he understood why. They'd

made a lot of promises when they were young. One of them was to buy that land one day, build their dream house and make babies beside that waterfall.

None of those promises had been kept.

"But you weren't supposed to be at the dance at all," she said.

"Our family trip out of town. Dad cut it short because of something that came up on one of his cases. As soon as we got home, I went to the dance looking for you."

"Right," she said, staring off as if picturing it in her head. "After the waterfall, we were heading back when one of my friends ran up to us, all excited about some guy asking her out. She wanted to tell me about it, so I promised I'd meet you back in the dance hall in a few minutes." She cleared her throat. "But that didn't happen. The next time I saw you, you were on a stretcher being taken into an ambulance. And my mother was yelling at me to come with her, that we had to go with Brian. The police were arresting him and she wanted us to follow him to the police station." Her haunted eyes met his. "I should have told her no. I'm so sorry, Colin. I made so many mistakes."

There was a lot they needed to discuss, one day, to clear the air between them. Their past, everything that had happened after the fire, was the elephant in the room that they'd never talked about. But late at night when they were both tired wasn't the time for that conversation.

"Let's get back to your mom. We were trying to see if she had an opportunity to start the fire."

She twisted her hands together. "Right. I'm guessing most of us could have gone to the barn during the dance if we'd wanted to. How do I prove whether my mom did or didn't go down there?"

He drummed his knuckles on his thigh, considering. "There's only one way I can think of that might prove where your mother was at the time of the fire. But you're not going to like it."

"Try me."

"Tell you what. I'm not even sure it's an option. Let me look into it first and see if I can work it out."

"Ah. One of those supersecret US Marshal types of things." She hid another yawn behind her hand. "If I weren't so tired, I'd argue with you to tell me right now. But honestly, even my curiosity isn't strong enough to keep me awake much longer." She stood and adjusted her shirt, which had ridden up around her hips. "Aren't you going to bed too?"

"You go ahead. I'll get the lights, have a quick look around to make sure things are secure."

She glanced at the windows behind him. "Oh. Okay. Well, good night, then." She started toward him, then stopped, looking uncertain. "Can I hug you? Your bruises—"

"Are pretty much gone. I'd hug you anyway." He stood and pulled her into his arms. It felt so good to hold her, especially since she'd been gone for over a week and he'd really never expected her to come back. He finally let her go only because he didn't trust himself to hold her any longer without kissing her. And kissing her would leave him aching for so much more.

Even if there had been no baggage between them, he didn't know if they'd ever be able to move past something far more tangible—his scars. The young man she'd made love with all those years ago wasn't the man standing before her today. And *that* was something they might never be able to overcome.

After she disappeared up the stairs, he pulled out his phone and sat down to call his father. Although Duncan had already broken the news to their parents that Peyton had come back—and had stirred up Colin's life again—Colin had put off making the same call. He knew there'd be no way to avoid telling them about getting shot once they started asking questions. Then he'd have to spend a good amount of time groveling for not telling them about it, even though he hadn't been seriously hurt and hadn't wanted to alarm them. Once he finished groveling, he'd have to answer even more personal questions, questions he wasn't prepared to answer. But if he was going to help Peyton get the answers that *she* needed about her mom, that conversation could no longer be avoided.

A quick look at his watch had him hesitating. His father was a night owl. But eleven thirty was late, even for him. Still, there was a chance he might still be up. Colin decided to risk it.

An hour later, he felt like he'd just gotten out of a boxing ring after twelve rounds and a knockout punch. Both of his parents had ended up on the call, tag-teaming each other in the interrogation like the pros they once were, when she'd been a prosecutor and he was a federal judge. In order to be forgiven for not keeping them in the loop about being shot, he'd had to promise to come up to their cabin for dinner for the next five consecutive Fridays, plus go to church with his mom on two

Sundays of her choosing. The sacrifice had been worth it. Because in return, his father was giving him exactly what he'd asked for.

The part of the discussion about Brian's escape had been the easy part. His parents knew how law enforcement worked. They knew not to push for any nonpublic information—which was pretty much just that four escaped convicts had killed a Memphis police officer and were on the run in the Gatlinburg area.

As for the heinous killings of three of those fugitives, so far Landry had been able to keep that out of the media. He hoped to keep it quiet until after the killer was caught. Colin readily agreed. Peyton certainly didn't need to have that gruesome detail in her head, and he had no intention of telling her. Some burdens were better *not* shared.

He stood, stretched and was about to round the coffee table to head to his room when one of the papers caught his attention—the police report on the single-car accident that had claimed the life of Peyton's mother. Thinking about the irony that she'd been killed so soon after being diagnosed with terminal cancer, he picked up the report and skimmed it.

It had been a rainy night. The roads were wet. Her car had lost control on a curve and slammed into a tree. The gas tank had been punctured, and the vehicle burst into flames. The body was burned beyond recognition. Her father had had her remains cremated and Peyton said they'd sprinkled her ashes within sight of the prison walls where Brian was being held. It had been an unusual request in her mother's will and Peyton hadn't wanted to comply. But her father had insisted that they follow her wishes. She'd adored her son and that was her way of being close to him.

He scrubbed his jaw and slowly sat back down.

Cars bursting into flames were common in action movies. But in reality, even in severe crashes, it was rare. Thankfully, so were sorority house fires, especially fatal ones. What had Peyton said earlier tonight about her mom? That she'd always had candles lit around the house, and a fire in the fireplace, even in the middle of summer. Peyton had called it an unhealthy fascination with fire.

A terrible suspicion struck him. He immediately discarded it as ludicrous, the kind of fantastical scheme that might appear in a movie.

Like a car exploding into flames?

He scooted forward and rummaged through the papers on the coffee table until he found the life insurance policy he'd seen earlier. Mrs. Sterling's death certificate was stapled to the policy. Grabbing it, he jogged to his office down the back hallway.

Twenty minutes later, he had the autopsy report on Molly Sterling sitting on the computer screen in front of him—and even more questions. Dozens of internet searches later, and a promise to give his next Tennessee Vols basketball home game ticket to a police officer working the night desk in Memphis, he had the phone number that he needed. And he wasn't about to wait until morning to make the call. If this incredibly remote, insane theory panned out, he needed to get that information to the marshals and Chief Landry, immediately.

He pulled out his phone and made the call. After five rings, it went to voice mail. He didn't leave a message. He hung up and called again, and again, and again. On the fifth try, the phone was answered on the first ring.

"What the hell do you want?" the sleepy voice demanded.

"Dr. Afton, sorry to wake you at this ridiculous hour. But this is extremely important. My name is—"

"I'm going to hang up and you're not going to call me back. Instead, you're going to call the medical examiner who's on call, which is *not* me."

"If you hang up, I *will* call you back. Like I said, I'm—"

"And I'll call 911 and report that someone's harassing—"

"If someone has metastatic cancer with tumors in the liver and brain, would that show up in an autopsy if the body was burned in a fire?"

The phone was silent for so long that Colin had to check to see whether the call had dropped. "Dr. Afton?"

"Who is this?"

Colin sighed. "I've been trying to tell you that I'm Deputy US Marshal Colin McKenzie. I'm assisting in the hunt for a wanted fugitive, Brian Sterling. While working that case, some questions came up that—"

"Wait, did you say Sterling?"

"I did."

"Any relation to Molly Sterling?"

"Brian is her son." Colin waited, but the line went silent again. "Dr. Afton?"

A loud sigh sounded through the phone. "I knew cutting corners would come back to bite me."

Colin straightened in his chair. "Cutting corners?"

"Give me five minutes. I'll call you back." The line clicked.

Chapter Eighteen

Peyton stepped off the bottom stair and paused when she saw her book bag sitting by the couch where she'd left it last night. Inside were the letters Colin had written her all those years ago. She'd meant to put the bag in her room until later, when the timing was better for a lengthy, extremely personal talk. Had he looked inside? Seen the letters?

"Morning." He rounded the corner from the hall behind the stairs holding a cup of coffee.

"Morning. I guess I owe you an apology for last night."

He stopped in front of her. "Why?"

"I shouldn't have left a mess in here. I should have picked up all my papers and photo albums." She glanced toward the coffee table—the now *empty* coffee table. "I guess you put them up for me somewhere?"

He followed her glance. "Oh. I took them to my office last night after you went to bed. I wanted to research a few things and didn't want to risk making too much noise out here." He motioned toward the book bag sitting in the floor. "I wasn't sure what you had in the bag and whether you wanted me to see it, so I left it alone."

Her cheeks heated. "Yes, well, it's nothing that I want to go into just yet. I'm guessing your research was about whatever you hinted at last night. Should we go to your office so you can show me what you found?" She stepped in that direction but he stopped her with a hand on her arm.

"That's not where you'll find what I was hinting at last night. We need to take a little drive."

"A drive?"

"About forty minutes, not far. I see you're showered and ready to start the day. Any objections to grabbing breakfast at a drive-through in town and hitting the road right now? Coffee's ready in the kitchen. You can take a mug with you."

"Have they…have they found Brian? Are we going to the police station?"

"Unfortunately, no. Let's get you some coffee and I'll explain on the way."

"Sounds like you're worried that I won't go if I know the destination ahead of time."

He gave her a crooked grin that made him look so young, her heart hurt.

"That's exactly what I'm afraid of. But you'll thank me later. Eventually. Maybe."

"Gee, you make it sound so appealing."

"Then you'll go?"

"Against my better judgment, I'll go."

"You're taking me *where*?"

Colin winced and glanced at a red-faced Peyton

glaring at him from the passenger seat of his truck. Thankfully he'd waited until she finished her fast-food sandwich before he broke the news. Otherwise, she'd have probably thrown it at him.

Her jaw set, she stared out the window as if judging the speed of the truck.

He hit the automatic door locks.

She rolled her eyes. "Really? You think I'm stupid enough to jump?"

"Angry enough, maybe."

Her shoulders slumped. "*Angry* isn't the right word. I'm…terrified. That they'll hate me. It's been ten years, Colin. After what my family has done to your family, after what I've done to you—"

"Hey, hey. You haven't done anything to me. Let that guilt go right now."

"You were burned. I wasn't there for—"

"Yeah, well. That's a discussion for another day, for you and me. Not you, me and my parents. It's none of their business. And this isn't a casual visit to reminisce and take a trip down memory lane either. It's a quest for the truth. So we can put all of this business behind us and get back to that conversation you and I need to have. Alone. All right?"

She leaned toward him and put her hand on his thigh. "All right. Thank you, Colin. I don't think I could have survived everything that's been happening if it weren't for you."

He swallowed and tried not to think about her warm hand sliding across his leg, or anywhere else. Out of desperation, he subtly shifted toward the door and she pulled her hand back.

"We'll get through this together," he said. "No worries."

She watched the trees passing by the window as he turned onto the narrow road that led up the last part of the mountain to his family home.

"I don't understand how going to see your parents is going to help with my quest for answers."

"People don't call Dad *the Mighty McKenzie* for nothing."

"I thought you didn't like that name. You felt it was derogatory."

He shrugged. "Depends on who's saying it, and their tone. It can be. On the other hand, it denotes a certain authority and respect within the legal community. During Brian's trial, your family resented my dad because even though he wasn't assigned to the case, he always seemed to know what was going on. Things pretty much went his way—which means my way, as a witness and, technically, a victim since I was burned."

Her glance flicked to his hands, then away. "Okay, and that will help us now, how?"

"Brian's case was important to Dad, for two reasons. Me. And you."

"Me? I don't understand."

He slowed for a particularly sharp curve. Once he was on a straightaway again, he glanced at her. "Don't you know, Peyton? I wasn't the only one who loved you back then. You were like a daughter to Mom and Dad. In the beginning, even with me telling them I saw Brian with that gas can, they did everything they could to prove he was innocent. Because he was your brother, because they wanted to help you."

She pressed a hand to her throat. "I never knew they tried to help."

"It wasn't like they were proud of it. In their eyes, they'd failed you. They felt there was nothing they could do for you after that, so they had to fully focus on getting me well and helping me through the ordeal of the trial."

She squeezed her eyes shut. "Getting you well. Colin, when you were burned, you actually wrote me sweet, wonderful, old-fashioned letters—"

"Stop."

She looked at him. "What?"

"We can talk about that later, okay? Let's focus on the case first."

She seemed like she wanted to argue, but she finally nodded. "Of course. Okay. I'm sorry."

He held out his hand toward her. She immediately threaded her fingers through his. He rested them on the seat between them.

"What I was trying to explain in my own clumsy way is that Dad maintained a thick file on Brian's case. It's obviously not the official case file, but it has copies of everything he could get his hands on. And more. He even hired a private investigator to see what he could find."

"I've seen the official case file, read transcripts even though I was there through the trial," she said. "I don't see how a file your father maintained, even with notes from a private investigator, would help answer my questions about my mom."

"Time stamps."

"What?"

He turned the truck down the last curve. The family cabin loomed in the distance, two stories of thick log walls perched on the edge of one of the highest peaks in the Smoky Mountains west of Gatlinburg.

"Pictures," he said, as he urged his truck up the last fifty yards of steep grade. "Dad has tons and tons of pictures from the dance, the paths, the waterfalls and the barn. He had the PI buy copies of every single picture he could get from nearly everyone who was there that night. I imagine he has way more pictures than either the prosecutor or the defense ever had."

He pulled the truck to a stop in one of the parking spaces his parents had paved for their large family. "No one ever suspected your mom. Ever. There wasn't any reason to. So no one, to my knowledge, has ever tried to create a timeline from those pictures to prove where she was at different times that evening."

Peyton chewed her bottom lip, her hand tightening on his as she stared up at the cabin. "You really think enough of the pictures have dates and times on them to be of any use? I don't remember setting dates and times very often on my pictures when I was younger."

He squeezed her hand and let go so he could get out of the truck, but he hesitated after popping open the door. "You underestimate the Mighty McKenzie. He had the PI print pictures from the actual photo cards in each camera, and write the dates and times from the metadata from those cards onto the back of each picture. That way, all of them have time stamps. And they should all be accurate."

For the first time in a long time, she gave him a smile that reached her eyes. "It will be such a relief to know, one way or the other. Thank you." Her gaze slid to the cabin. "It hasn't changed much over the years. It's still...huge."

He laughed. "I suppose it is. They needed a lot of space for four boys to run around. Mom had the kitchen renovated a few years ago, had new beams put in to carry the weight of the second story so she could have a wall knocked down. Open concept and all that. There might be a few new pieces of furniture here and there. But overall, it's pretty much the same."

He hopped down from the truck and headed around to her side. After opening the door, he reached in to help her down. Her soft hands gripped his shoulders like a lifeline. It was then that he saw the fear in her eyes and realized the depth of her concern over the reception she'd receive from his parents.

"It will be okay." He tried to reassure her. "I promise." She was so tiny compared to him. He couldn't help grinning when he lifted her down and set her on her feet.

She frowned up at him as if reading his mind. "No short jokes."

"No tall jokes."

She blinked, then laughed. "Deal."

He kept her hand tightly in his and led her to the door. It opened as soon as they got there, which told him his mother had been watching for them. She stood in the opening, smiling through her tears as she engulfed Peyton in a tight hug.

"Welcome home, daughter," she said, still holding Peyton in her arms. "We've missed you so much."

Tears were streaming down Peyton's face when Colin's mother finally let her go. Peyton gave him a help-less look, obviously not sure what to do. But his mother was already taking charge, grabbing Peyton's hand and tugging her into the house.

"Come along, Peyton. Dad's waiting in his office. Let's get all of that business stuff out of the way so we can chat about that lovely store of yours downtown. Peyton's Place, right? I was there yesterday. Just ador-able. Love the croissants."

Colin imagined that Peyton wasn't looking forward to that conversation, to telling his mother that the store belonged to someone else now. His mother never slowed, pulling her through the family room toward the opposite end of the house. Peyton glanced at Colin over her shoulder, a bemused expression on her face.

He grinned and nodded his encouragement. The tears had stopped. And he'd be eternally grateful to his mother for her warm welcome of Peyton. It was ex-actly what she'd needed. But then, his mother always seemed to know what everyone needed.

She stopped at the open door to Colin's father's of-fice, her arm around Peyton's shoulders. "William, get over here and welcome our daughter home."

"I'm coming, I'm coming," his father called out.

Colin stopped behind Peyton, not quite touching, but close enough so that he knew she'd be able to feel his warmth, know he was there for her no matter what.

He needn't have worried.

As soon as his father stopped in front of her and opened his arms, she let out a sob and stepped into his embrace.

Chapter Nineteen

Peyton couldn't help feeling intimidated sitting across the desk from Colin's distinguished-looking father, while Colin stood in front of the wall of bookshelves behind his dad, watching her with that intense gaze of his. Whether they realized it or not, the two of them presented a powerful united front that had her feeling defensive even though she knew they both only wanted to help. Maybe it was her usual Sterling family guilt that was making her feel that way.

She forced her attention back to the pictures she was flipping through, one of many stacks that had been taken from the dozens of folders spread out on the desk. The mass of information that McKenzie senior had accumulated on Brian's case made the official police file seem like an abridged summary.

There was a picture of her mom, wearing that awful forest-print dress Peyton had hated. She'd joked that her mother would blend in with the wood-paneled walls and no one would even see her. Her mom's feelings had been hurt—it was a brand-new dress and she'd loved it. Peyton had had to do a quick one-eighty and pretend she'd been kidding in order to appease her mom and make her smile again.

The dress really was hideous.

Another picture was one that she knew well. It had been the smoking gun at the trial, an out-of-focus snapshot of a figure fleeing into the woods, with the beginnings of flames barely visible in the lower window of the barn to his left. The figure's back was to the camera, but it was definitely a male. He had short dark hair, jeans and a tucked-in shirt—which described *most* of the boys at the dance. But *this figure* was holding a gas can.

The prosecution had argued that it proved Brian had set the fire. The defense argued that it proved someone else had set the fire. Peyton had stared at that shadowy figure for hours and still couldn't swear that it was, or wasn't, her brother. Of course, if it was, his argument to her at the high school was that he'd been taking that can out to *prevent* a fire. When she'd shared that information with Colin during the phone call on her drive to Memphis, he'd flat-out said he didn't believe it. She had to agree with him that it sounded weak, a desperate attempt to explain the unexplainable.

She flipped to the next picture, then the next and the next. She and Colin were in quite a few of them, her in a minidress that hugged every curve. Him looking sexier than humanly possible in jeans that hugged his lean hips and tight rear end, his collared shirt half tucked in as he swung her around the dance floor. She curled her fingers against the urge to trace the lines of his arms. That had been the last time she saw him in short sleeves.

She set the first stack of pictures aside and stared at the many more stacks she had yet to go through.

"Everything okay?" Colin asked.

She shrugged. "Real life cases sure aren't like TV, are they? All that CSI stuff, fingerprints, DNA. Brian's case has none of that. There's no black and white, only gray, and so many ways to look at what little evidence there is. I wouldn't have all the questions I have today if there was hard evidence to rely on. But his case is almost entirely circumstantial. It's just so frustrating."

His father waved toward the other side of the room, where a row of cherrywood filing cabinets fit end to end beneath the wall of windows overlooking the mountains.

"Those cabinets hold my entire life's work, my personal notes on thousands of cases. Probably eighty percent are based almost *exclusively* on circumstantial evidence. Real life doesn't always come with videos, pictures, DNA and fingerprints. That's why we rely so heavily on old-fashioned police work—investigations, interviews and eyewitnesses."

"But eyewitnesses aren't reliable," she argued. "I'm no expert but even I've seen documentaries showing how two people can see the same thing from different vantage points and have completely different accountings of what happened."

Colin straightened away from the bookshelf behind him. "Which is exactly why law enforcement insists on having corroborating witnesses. In your brother's case, there were five people who agreed they saw Brian with that gas can near the barn. Including me. I knew your brother for years. Do you really think I'd swear under oath that I saw him if there was *any* doubt in my mind?"

She slowly shook her head. "No. I don't. But it was dark—"

"Not right by the barn where I saw him. Party lights were strung throughout the property, lighting up the paths and buildings. Remember? Brian ran out, and the barn went up in flames right after."

All three of them went silent, no doubt thinking about Colin running into that inferno to make sure no one was inside. He'd found two people already knocked unconscious by a burning, fallen timber. He hadn't hesitated to help them, regardless of the danger to himself.

Peyton cleared her throat and tried to get the conversation back on track. "I know that Brian claimed at the school over a week ago that he was indeed the one carrying that gas can—supposedly to prevent the fire. But since we're playing devil's advocate and trying to prove the truth, I'll argue that you can't swear it was him since you only saw him from the back. You saw a young man from behind, running away from you. It could have been anyone."

"I could see *you* from any angle, Peyton, and I'd know it was you."

Her face heated. She refused to look at his father. "I thought we were here to determine my mother's whereabouts during the dance, not rehash where Brian was."

Colin waved toward the other pictures and folders. "We are. But Dad and I both thought you might want to look at all of the evidence first, everything he has, to form a complete picture of what happened that night. If you go into a case with preconceived notions, you're likely to miss an important clue that could end up solving the entire puzzle. And as you just pointed out, Brian's recent version of events is the polar opposite of what he's claimed all these years. I don't think we can trust him."

"No arguments here." She rubbed her hands across her jeans.

His father pushed himself to standing. "How about I leave you two alone to go through all this without a federal judge looking over your shoulders?"

"You don't have to leave," Peyton said. "You're not making me feel uncomfortable."

He smiled. "I appreciate that. But I'm hankering for another one of those delicious croissants that Margaret picked up at your store yesterday. I'll check back later."

He left the room and closed the door.

Peyton chewed her bottom lip. "I suppose now isn't the time to tell him that Joan buys those croissants from another bakery across town and repackages them."

Colin grinned. "Probably not." He opened the top desk drawer and pulled out a small magnifying glass. "For the pictures, just in case. Sometimes little details escape the naked eye and might be important." He sat down across from her. "How do you want to do this? I get the impression that you're not interested in reviewing all the folders."

"Is it that obvious?"

"It *is* a lot to sort through. We can focus entirely on the pictures for now, build a timeline off that and then determine our next steps. Sound like a plan?"

"Sounds perfect. How do we start?"

He opened the drawer again, this time pulling out

some legal pads and pens and setting them in the middle of the desk. "Divide and conquer. I suggest we separate any pictures of your mom to one stack, and pictures of Brian to another. Any pictures of the scene itself—the barn before it burned down, and the immediate area surrounding it—go in a third stack."

She nodded, then picked up the infamous smoking gun picture. "Where would this one go? It's by the barn, but supposedly this is a picture of Brian."

"Fourth stack. Undecided. Once we have only the pictures we're most interested in, we use the time stamps on the back of each one to put them in order."

"Timeline, right?"

He smiled. "Timeline."

They each took a stack of pictures and started sorting.

Even with the two of them culling through the pictures, it took over two hours to finish.

Peyton stood and crossed to the window, stretching her aching back from being stooped over for so long. "Sorry I wasted your time. I should have known better than to expect school kids to take enough pictures with the chaperones in them to do any good."

He joined her by the window and rested his hip against one of the filing cabinets. "It wasn't a waste of time. You have to go down a lot of roads in an investigation to determine whether they're worth going down. It had to be done."

"What else is there? How else can we fill the gaps in the timeline?"

He scrubbed his jaw. "I hate to say it. But we're probably back to looking through Dad's entire file to find another thread to pull."

She groaned. "I don't think I'm up for that. It'll take a week to go through everything."

"Probably."

"How are you even working on this with me at this point? I'm not going to get you fired for missing work am I?"

He hesitated. "I'm not working this on my own time anymore. I'm officially assigned to Brian's case, have been since the day you went back to Memphis." He waved toward the desk. "This, reviewing the old case files, is all part of that."

"Oh. Well, then, that's good. I guess. But I thought there was a conflict of interest, that you couldn't work on this because..."

"Because of our past?"

She nodded.

"My boss finally had to accept that there was no way to keep me from looking into everything, whether I was on my own or not. He decided to make it official. Besides, since your encounter at the school, things have... heated up. Catching Brian has become job number one. Pretty much everyone in law enforcement around here is helping, one way or another."

"You said catching *Brian*. You meant catching Brian and the three other escapees, right?"

He hesitated. "Right."

She put her hands on her hips. "Is there something you're not telling me?"

He straightened. "There are always things in investigations that can't be shared with civilians."

"Civilians? I'm a part of this, not just a civilian."

"There's no difference in the eyes of law enforcement." He waved toward his father's desk, at the folders spread across the top. "You've already been given far more access to information than most people ever would. I'm walking a thin line here. I can't do more than I already have."

She crossed her arms. "Do you always have to be so logical and make perfect sense? You make it impossible for me to be mad at you."

He grinned. "And here I was expecting a big fight. You surprise me."

"I'll save the big fight for later. I'm sure you're bound to really tick me off at some point."

"No doubt." He chuckled. "I guess we're done here then. Do you want to stay and visit awhile or—"

"If I have a choice, I'd rather go back to your house. I'm just not ready to be social, you know? With everything going on. That is, if it won't upset your parents."

"They'll understand. Just give me a few minutes. I haven't seen them in a while and I'm sure they'll have a few more questions for me before we go." He strode out the door and disappeared down the hall.

She looked back at the desk, the messy piles of folders and pictures scattered everywhere. They looked so out of place in the otherwise pristine office. She headed to the desk and started straightening everything into logical piles. But since she wasn't sure which folders to put the various pictures in, she arranged all of them in neat stacks in front of the folders. The smoking gun picture ended up on top of one group. A picture of her mom in that awful forest-print dress sat on top of the grouping beside it.

She couldn't resist picking up the controversial picture one more time and staring at the fleeing figure with the gas can.

Is that you, Brian? Are you carrying that gas can because you started the fire, or were trying to prevent one? Have I been defending you all these years even though you're guilty? Is Colin right?

She glanced at the picture of her mom, then picked it up.

Or have you been the culprit all along, Mom? Are you responsible for hurting Colin? Did you let your son go to prison for your crime?

As usual, no answers came to her. Would she ever really know what had happened? She set the picture down, glancing from one to the other, her mom in the ugly dress to the figure with the gas can. She frowned and looked back at her mom again. Something wasn't quite right. Something was…off. She looked at the other picture, then back again, several times. She sucked in a breath, then grabbed both pictures and ran to the window. Tilting them up to the sunlight, she overlapped them a few inches.

Then she saw it.

The little detail she'd missed all these years, that everyone had missed, because the picture was so dark and blurry. There was no reason to think anything of it, and she probably never would have, if she hadn't seen it next to the other picture.

Laughter sounded from down the hall, followed by the clink of dishes. She could hear Colin's deep voice as he said something to his parents. His mom laughed again, probably at some joke he'd made or a funny memory he'd shared. Such a happy family, so *normal*. And she'd brought such turmoil into their lives. She'd been right before, when she'd said her whole life was a lie.

She studied the pictures again. It was such a tiny detail. Could she be wrong? She needed to be absolutely sure before telling Colin what she'd found. Because it changed everything. She crossed to the desk and had just picked up the small magnifying glass that Colin's father had set out when she heard footsteps coming down the hall toward the room. She whirled around, looking for her purse, then remembered she hadn't brought it. She turned her back to the door and shoved the small magnifying glass and two pictures down her cleavage into her bra.

The footsteps stopped. "Peyton? Ready to go?"

She fastened another button on her blouse, then forced a smile and turned around. "Ready."

Chapter Twenty

Peyton headed into the house with Colin, but paused in the back hallway instead of going into the main room.

She motioned toward his office door. "Do you mind if I borrow your office for a few minutes? I want to take another look at my albums while the pictures from your dad's files are still fresh in my mind." She crossed her fingers behind her back. Not that she was really lying. She did want to look at the albums again. But that wasn't the main reason she wanted a few minutes to herself.

"Sure, take all the time you need. But I'm hungry. How does a ham and cheese sandwich with lemonade sound?"

"It's only eleven. A bit early for lunch, isn't it?"

He rubbed his stomach. "Second breakfast."

She put her hands on her hips. "Second breakfast? Like the tiny hobbits have in *The Lord of the Rings*? I don't suppose that's another unsubtle attempt to tease me about my vertical stature?"

"I'm sure I don't know what you mean." He winked and strode past the stairs toward the kitchen.

"I like mustard and mayo on mine," she called out.

"You got it."

She smiled and pulled the pictures and magnifying

glass out of her bra as she hurried into his office. After clicking on his desk lamp, she bent over and held both the pictures close to the light, studying them. It didn't take long to confirm that she hadn't been mistaken. She put the pictures down on top of a folder and slumped into the desk chair.

What next? What else was lurking in her family's deep dark closets? And how many more times would she have to stand in the firing line and take another cannon to her heart? She was vaguely surprised she wasn't crying her eyes out again. But the urge to cry just wasn't there. She'd gone numb at this point. Thank God for small favors.

She had to tell Colin. Might as well rip off the Band-Aid and get it over with. She picked up the pictures, then noticed the neat printing on the folder label beneath them: Autopsy Results—Corrected: Molly Sterling. Why would Colin have an autopsy report on her mother? Setting her two pictures aside, she was about to flip open the folder when the label on the one beneath it had her drawing a sharp breath: Autopsy Results and Ballistics: Benjamin Sterling. Her father's autopsy report. She'd never seen a copy before, had never even thought to ask for one. Why did Colin have it? How in the world were both of her parents' autopsies relevant to the research on Brian? To the search for him and his fellow escapees?

Her hands shook as she took both of the folders and headed to the office couch to read them.

COLIN HUMMED "Boulevard of Broken Dreams" as he inventoried everything he'd set out on the kitchen island.

Bread, check. Although nothing as fresh and delicious as he knew Peyton could bake. Ham, check. Provolone cheese, check. He remembered she liked that. Mayo, check. Mustard, check. He didn't remember her mustard preference so he'd gone with spicy brown since that's what he liked. They'd always had a lot of the same likes and dislikes.

He'd promised lemonade, but the pitcher in the refrigerator was almost empty. He checked the pantry. There were fresh green apples, navel oranges, baking potatoes. No lemons. A twelve-pack of lemon-lime soda caught his eye. A poor substitute for fresh-squeezed lemonade, but at least it was in the same flavor category. He grabbed a couple of cans and set them on the island before filling some glasses with ice.

Now, all he had to do was slap the sandwiches together and—

He straightened, a piece of cheese dangling between his fingers. Peyton was in his office. To look at her albums. The last time he'd been in the office was early this morning making folders and printing out copies of—

Oh, no. Please, please, no.

He tossed the cheese on one of the plates and sprinted to his office, catching himself against the door frame.

Peyton was sitting on the couch in front of the bookshelves, her hands resting on two closed folders in her lap. Her face was alarmingly pale. And when she finally looked up at him, her calm exterior was belied by the pain in her tortured gaze.

Colin swallowed against the tightness in his throat and knelt on the floor in front of her. "Peyton, sweetheart. I'm so sor—"

"When were you going to tell me that my mother might still be alive? And how long were you going to let me believe that you'd shot my father, when Brian's the one who killed him?"

PEYTON SAT CROSS-LEGGED on the couch facing Colin with both of the folders in her lap. He sat sideways on the other end, his right arm resting along the back of the couch, one leg drawn up, the other stretched out in front of him.

She held up the folder with her father's name on it. "Let's get the easy one over with first. This is dated the day after I went to Memphis. Why didn't you tell me that ballistics tests prove the bullet that killed my father came from the gun that I took from Brian at the high school?"

He opened his mouth to respond, but Peyton held up a hand to stop him. "And don't you dare say you just wanted to protect me."

He closed his mouth.

"Seriously?" she asked. "You were trying to protect me? Again?"

He held his hands out in a conciliatory gesture. "You love your brother. I didn't want to add this to the burden you're already bearing when it comes to him."

"You'd rather I just go on believing that *you* shot him?"

"What's the point in rehashing the event and making you relive that pain all over again?"

"That's just another way of saying you were trying to protect me."

His jaw tightened and he crossed his arms over his chest.

Peyton let out a long sigh. "Okay. Well. I know you did what you felt was right, even though I *completely* disagree with your decision. Knowing that my brother killed my father…" She ruthlessly tamped down her emotions before she could continue. "That's a pretty important thing to know. If he could do something like that, and lie to my face about it when we spoke at the high school, he's capable of anything. My eyes are wide open now when it comes to my brother."

"You're handling this a lot better than I probably would have in your position," he admitted.

She scoffed. "I think what you meant to say is that you're astonished that I'm not drowning in a puddle of tears right now."

"That's not what I—"

"It's okay. I get it. I've been a nervous wreck ever since Brian showed up in my kitchen. And I've been crying so much I should invest in a tissue company. But I'm stronger than I look, and way stronger than I've been acting lately." She held up the second folder. "And I'm going to do my level best to hold it together while you answer my questions about this. But it's a lot to take in, so no promises."

His gaze flicked to the second folder in her lap, his brows knitting with worry. But, to his credit, he didn't try once again to convince her to let it go and ignore what she'd read.

"A lot of this is medical jargon over my head, so I'm not sure I got it all. You said there was an issue with the coroner, that he didn't perform his due diligence when conducting the autopsy on my mother." She held the folder out toward him. "Explain it to me. Please."

His reluctance was obvious in his expression, but he leaned forward and took the folder from her. When he didn't open it, she fisted her hands in frustration.

"Are you really going to make me go to Chief Landry or another marshal to ask them to explain this to me?"

"No." He pitched the folder onto the couch between them. "But I don't need to look at the reports to answer your questions. I called the coroner initially because it didn't sit right that your mom's car caught on fire in the accident. That's rare. And as you'd already pointed out, fire seems to crop up a lot in relation to your mom, from the sorority house fire onward. What I discovered is that the coroner was overworked and had a backlog of cases. He made a judgment call that your mom's case didn't seem suspicious, that it was simply a tragic accident. He skipped steps. He didn't pull dental records or try to test DNA because there was only one person in the car, the vehicle was registered to your mom and the victim was wearing jewelry that your father identified as belonging to her. Her purse was also in the car, half burned, with credit cards and her driver's license inside."

She held her hands out. "Makes sense to me. Honestly, I'd assume it was her too."

"As the coroner, he can't assume anything. In a case like this especially, where the body was, forgive me, burned beyond recognition, it's his duty to perform medical tests to verify the victim's identity. After I spoke to him, I strongly encouraged him to pull the

X-rays that he took during the autopsy and get dental records to compare—"

"Strongly encouraged?" She couldn't help smiling, if only a little. "I'll bet you had his career and future pension flashing in front of his eyes."

He returned her smile. "Possibly." His smile faded. "Peyton, the woman in the car wasn't your mother."

She'd read that in the report, but hearing it out loud seemed to suck the oxygen from the room. She wrapped her arms around her middle, nausea coiling in her stomach. If her mom hadn't been in the car, then another woman died in her place.

"Go on," she whispered, her throat so tight, she could barely speak. "Just say it. All of it."

His look of sympathy was almost her undoing. She clasped her hands in her lap and waited like a prisoner on death row watching the minutes tick away to midnight, hoping for the phone to ring but knowing that it won't.

"The coroner was able to get dental records overnight and did the comparison that he should have done originally. That proved the woman in the car wasn't your mother. But there aren't any missing persons cases in Memphis or the surrounding counties that seem like good candidates to be the victim. As for whether the car was tampered with to cause the accident, the car was crushed at a junkyard, so it can't be reexamined. However, the police did a thorough job of examining it the first time and I'm confident with their findings— that the car was in good working order before the crash. Based on that, and the lack of missing persons cases that I mentioned, I'm inclined to think the simplest scenario is the one that makes sense here. Someone robbed your mom and stole her car, then paid the ultimate price for their crimes."

He seemed to be waiting for her to say something, maybe to ask the next obvious question. But she didn't. She couldn't. Just holding herself together was taking all her energy.

"As for your mom," he continued, "that's open for speculation. The memorial service was over three months ago. If she's alive, one would expect that she'd have come forward, maybe to say she was carjacked or something. Since that hasn't happened, there are two logical possibilities. Either she was…murdered…by the person who took her car, or—"

"She's alive and wants people to think that she's dead," she managed to whisper.

"Yes."

"Is there…" She cleared her throat. "Is there any chance that if my mom really is alive, and hiding somewhere, for whatever reason, that the woman in her car…that my mom…" She couldn't say it, couldn't wrap her mind around it. But she had to know. She gave him a helpless look, hoping he'd understand what she was asking.

"You want to know whether your mom murdered the woman who was found in the car?"

She pursed her lips and nodded.

"The answer to that is complicated. There are extensive sketches and photographs from the police report that clearly indicate the car crashed into the tree and then caught on fire. And even though fire destroys evidence, the fire didn't completely consume the car. It was put out quickly enough to preserve enough clues for the police to piece together a few things. For example, there's no evidence that anyone besides the driver was in the car at the time of the accident. Also, the doors were jammed shut. And probably the most telling detail of all is that the driver had soot in her lungs at the time of the autopsy."

She covered her mouth. "Oh no."

He grimaced. "Yeah. I know. She was breathing when the car caught on fire. Hopefully she passed out and didn't suffer. Taking everything I just said into account, we know that she wasn't killed and placed in the car as part of some elaborate scheme. She was driving the car and wrecked it, and suffered horrible consequences as a result. Your mother probably had nothing to do with her death."

"Probably. I hope you're right. That would be one thing I could be thankful for. But that means either my mom was—" she twisted her hands together "—murdered, the victim of a carjacking. Or what? She decided when her car was taken that she'd take advantage of it? Use the opportunity to disappear? Why would she do that? She was dying of cancer. Given her prognosis, if she is alive and not undergoing treatment, she doesn't have much longer to live. So why fake her death?"

"I haven't been able to come up with any viable theories on that just yet. The only thing I can think of, and that's really thin, is that she wanted to spare her family the ordeal of watching her waste away from her disease. Maybe she thought it was a kinder way to say goodbye. A clean break. But regardless of the reason for disappearing, she'd still need money to live on. She'd need food, somewhere to stay, pain pills to help make her more comfortable."

"That wouldn't be a problem. Mom had her own money, separate from Dad, for as long as I can remember. It's just how they did things. Yes, she was helping pay Brian's legal fees. But she'd never give up all of her savings for him, or anyone else. I can totally see her stashing extra money away over the years, like from the grocery budget or clothing allowance, and building up a good nest egg. Plus, Dad had his faults, but being stingy wasn't one of them. Any time Mom asked for money, if he had it, he gave it to her." She shifted on the couch and rested her arm across the back like he was doing. "What happens next from a law-enforcement perspective, as far as my mom is concerned?"

"Quite a bit. The coroner has to revoke your mom's death certificate since the body in the car wasn't hers. Memphis police have already opened a missing persons report on your mom."

"Wow. Either you woke up a ton of people last night to get all of this rolling, or you were super busy this morning before I ever got out of bed."

He smiled. "A little of both. Memphis PD is also reopening the investigation around the crash to include the timeline leading up to it. The goal is to search for witnesses and to track your mother's movements to figure out where she was last seen. They've got a good team up there. I'm confident they'll do everything they can to figure out what happened to her."

"Thank you, Colin. I appreciate you explaining everything. I don't guess any of this helps with the search for Brian and his fellow escapees though."

His hand tensed against the back of the couch. If her hand hadn't been close to his, she wouldn't have even caught the movement.

"There's something else, isn't there?" she asked. "Something you're not telling me, about Brian? And the other fugitives?"

He scrubbed his jaw and straightened. "Our sandwiches. I left the lunch meat on the counter. I should put it away before it—"

"Colin. Please. No more surprises. Let's level with each other here and now and not hold anything else back."

He rested his forearms on his knees and turned his head To look at her. "Each other? There's something about the case that *you're* not telling *me*?"

She hesitated, then nodded. "It's the reason I came in here to begin with. I needed a few minutes to look at something, to be absolutely sure before I told you. But let's be clear. I was going to tell you." She smiled. "Unlike someone else I know around here." Her attempt at infusing a teasing tone into her gibe didn't even coax a smile out of him.

He stood and crossed to the window that looked over the backyard and the acres of green grass and trees that seemed to go on forever. She'd admired that same view many times from the windows off the kitchen since coming to his home. The longer he stood there, the more nervous and full of dread she became. She smoothed her hands on her jeans and crossed to the window, stopping a few feet behind him.

"I've been badgering you all morning," she said. "Time for me to woman up, I guess, and tell you what I've discovered." She moved to the desk to grab the pictures she'd left on top of one of the albums.

"Peyton."

His somber tone had her turning around. He had his hands in his pockets and was leaning against the windowsill, his long legs braced out in front of him. "We aren't searching for the three fugitives anymore who escaped with your brother. We found their bodies the same day you spoke to Brian at the high school."

"Bodies? You found their…bodies?"

"They were burned."

She pressed her hand to her throat. "Oh my God. To keep the police from knowing it was them? How did they die? Were they shot? Oh, Colin. Please don't tell me that Brian shot them right before meeting me, with the same gun that I took from him." She shuddered at the thought of touching the gun that had been used to kill her father and possibly three other men.

He slowly shook his head. "They weren't shot."

"I don't understand. You said the bodies were…" She read the truth in his eyes, and shuddered. "Oh, dear Lord above. Who would… Brian? You're telling me he—"

"No. The timing wasn't right. He couldn't have set the fire. Someone else did, at the same time that he was being chased through the woods miles away by some marshals. We believe that Brian is working with someone else, and that second person is the one who killed the escapees. It could explain a lot. A partner could have arranged transportation, picked them up after they escaped the van, gave them money, had places picked out ahead of time where they could hide to evade the searchers. It can also explain where the gun came from that was used to shoot Jennings and your father."

"Wait. The gun I took from Brian didn't belong to Officer Jennings?"

"His gun was still in his holster when they found him. He never had a chance to draw."

"One more lie to chalk up to Brian. I should have known. You think this…partner…is the one who killed the fugitives?"

"I don't think one person could have kept them compliant to allow him to tie them up to a tree. Someone must have held a gun on them while someone else tied them up. Then the one with the gun left, and the partner…took care of loose ends."

"Brian was the one with the gun," she said, her voice hoarse.

"I believe so, yes."

She turned back toward the desk and slowly lowered herself into the chair. She picked up the two pictures that she'd taken from McKenzie senior's office and set them in front of her. "Who do you think his partner is?"

"I have a theory."

She let out a ragged breath. "Me too." She held the first photo up in the air. "If you take a fresh look at the smoking gun picture, you'll see the window in the barn isn't quite square. That's because the lower-left corner has a small piece of fabric behind it, inside the barn. It looks almost exactly like the wood on the barn itself, so it's nearly impossible to notice unless you're looking for it." She held up the second picture, the one of her mother wearing the forest-print dress. "That fabric exactly matches the pattern on the dress my mother was wearing the night of the dance." She smiled sadly. "I think we both know who started the barn fire now. And we have our answer about whether my mother is alive or dead."

Chapter Twenty-One

Several times throughout the day, Colin headed to the stairs, determined to talk Peyton into coming down from her room. But each time he put his foot on the bottom step, he stopped. She hadn't been angry at him when she'd left his office. She'd been sad, confused, overwhelmed. And she'd told him she needed some time to make sense of everything she'd learned, to figure out her next steps.

He wanted more than anything for her to figure out those next steps *with him*, to let him be there for her. But she wasn't ready to lean on him, to lessen her burdens by sharing them, to work through their hopes and fears together, like they'd once done. The idea that she might never be ready terrified him. Because the one constant in his life, the one thing he'd realized since she'd come back, was that he'd been fooling himself thinking he'd gotten over her. He could never get over her. He loved her more now than ever before. And he didn't know how he was going to survive if she walked out of his life again.

One thing was certain, he couldn't keep pacing the floor all day. He had to get out of here, work off some of this nervous energy. Take his mind off Peyton. Take his mind off an investigation that kept opening up wounds from the past but never seemed to lead to a resolution.

He strode through the family room, through the kitchen and out the door. Ignoring the stairs, he leaped off the back deck and took off at a run, not stopping until he reached the workshop building.

He unlocked the door and flung it open, then propped it back with a piece of wood to get some airflow inside. Even with shorts on because of the heat, he was already sweating. The long sleeves didn't help. And with Peyton upstairs and showing no sign of coming down, there was no reason to give himself heatstroke. He took off his shirt and flung it on a workbench. Then he headed straight to the broken tractor, determined to finally wrestle it into submission.

Several hours later, the beast was purring like a cat drunk on catnip. Not long after that, both ATVs had a fresh oil change and a new fuel filter, and were shined up and ready for future treks over the mountain to check on his newest acquisition, the tract of land he'd had his eye on for years but that had only come available a few months ago. But since he didn't want to be out of sight of the house just in case Brian—and his mother—decided to pay a visit, he spent the remaining daylight hours patching and painting over the bullet holes Brian's last visit had made in the siding on the workshop building.

The light sensor had the bug light behind the house flickering on when he set his dirty boots on the deck and headed inside. He used his shirt to wipe the sweat from his chest and arms as he strode through the house to his bedroom to take a much-needed shower.

He stepped inside his bedroom, and froze. Peyton was standing in profile on the other side of the bed, looking out the window into the side yard.

"There you are," she said as she began to turn around. "I've been look—"

Her eyes widened and she pressed her hands to her throat, staring at his chest. "Oh, Colin. Oh no, *Colin*."

He'd learned to expect this type of reaction from other people. He hadn't expected it from her, though, not after everything they'd been through the past few weeks. What a fool he'd been to think that she could love him enough to overlook the physical, love him for who he was, not the scarred shell he'd become.

The urge to cover himself was nearly overwhelming as her horrified gaze traveled over the ridges and dips that covered his chest and arms. But he wasn't about to cower and act ashamed. He'd saved two people's lives. It had cost him dearly. But given the choice, he'd do it all over again. Life was a precious gift, worth any sacrifice. Even if it meant sacrificing the love of his life.

"Colin," she choked out, still not looking up at his face.

He gritted his teeth. "If you're through staring in disgust at my scars, I need to take a shower."

Her gaze flew to his. "What? No, I didn't mean—"

"Excuse me." He strode past her into the master bathroom and considered it a victory that he managed to shut the door without slamming it.

PEYTON ZIPPED THE bag of freshly baked croissants closed and set them on the kitchen island. With Colin gone for several hours now, she'd filled the time baking, and had definitely gone with a chocolate theme. Three dozen chocolate fudge cookies sat in another bag. A devil's food cake took up the middle, resting on a plain dinner plate covered with plastic wrap since she couldn't find a cake keeper in Colin's kitchen. Yet another sheet of chocolate chip cookies, still too warm to put away, sat cooling on the opposite end of the island.

The oven beeped, letting her know it was preheated again for her next venture—a homemade Dutch apple pie. Well, almost homemade. She'd been forced to make the crust from a few cans of ready-made biscuit dough. But she'd almost wept when she'd seen the bag of fresh-picked apples sitting on a shelf in the pantry. Not because it meant she could make a decent pie. But because she remembered how much Colin had always loved apples, green not red. And how much fun they'd had together picking them at the same orchard every summer.

She slid the pie into the oven and set the timer. Then washed her hands in the sink.

"Someone's been busy. Again."

She whirled around. Colin stood in the opening to the family room. His expression was guarded, his gaze flitting over the food on top of the island. He was fully dressed, once again wearing jeans and a long-sleeved shirt that buttoned at his wrists. Only his feet were bare.

"I, ah, hope you don't mind that I took over your kitchen. I tend to bake when I'm—"

"Upset. I know." He leaned against the wall. "I'm sorry about earlier. I should have kept my shirt on when I came inside. I assumed you'd still be upstairs. I shouldn't have."

She blinked. "I don't...are you seriously apologizing to me?"

He moved into the kitchen. "Not everyone can handle it, seeing the scars. I should have been more careful." His hand hovered over one of the chocolate chip cookies cooling on the baking sheet. "Do you mind?"

"What? No, of course not. It's your food, after all. Please. Take whatever you want, I..." She swallowed as he took a bite of a cookie, then closed his eyes, a look of pleasure washing over his handsome face.

He opened his eyes. "That's probably the best chocolate chip cookie I've ever had. I'll bet it was a favorite at your store." He popped the rest of the cookie into his mouth and crossed to the sink.

She moved out of the way so he could wash his hands.

"Glad you liked it."

He dried his hands on the dish towel and leaned down to look in the oven. "Is that an apple pie?"

"I hope you don't mind. I used most of the apples in your pantry. Were you saving them for something?"

He hung the dish cloth on a hook by the sink, then rested his hip against the counter. "Not particularly. I've told you before, you're welcome to use anything in the kitchen. No exceptions."

"Thanks. Um, Colin. About before. I think you misunderstood. I wasn't—"

"Don't worry about it. I really should be used to that kind of reaction by now. Even my brothers give me a startled look if I take off my shirt while working outside." He smiled, but the smile didn't quite reach his eyes. "Forget it. Have you eaten dinner? I took a nap after my shower and woke up starving." He yanked open the refrigerator and peered inside. "I never did make those sandwiches earlier. I could still throw together some—"

"Stop it." She leaned past him and shut the refrigerator door. "We need to talk." She flattened a palm against his chest, feeling the ridges of scars beneath the material. "We need to talk about *this*." She tapped his shirt.

He plucked her hand off him, his eyes darkening. "Turns out I'm not as hungry as I thought." He moved past her and strode out of the kitchen.

She hurried after him. "Colin, please. Stop."

"Good night, Peyton." He passed the stairs, heading to his bedroom.

She spotted her book bag by the couch and grabbed it. Colin shoved his bedroom door open. In desperation, she lifted the bag into the air and flipped it upside down. The letters tumbled out, thumping against the coffee table and plunking onto the hardwood floor in a sea of white, like flat, rectangular snow.

He stopped and looked over his shoulder. His gaze traveled over envelope after envelope, his brow furrowed in confusion. "What are you doing?"

She tossed the now empty bag onto one of the couches. "They're from you, the letters you sent me after the fire. All sixty-two of them. Until my father's death, until I found these hidden in the attic, I never knew you'd tried to contact me after the fire. My father refused to let me call you. He took my phone away. And he swore you never once tried to even send me a text."

His face reddened as he turned to face her. "And you believed him?"

She felt her own face flushing with heat. "He was my *father*. I had no reason *not* to believe him."

"No reason except that I loved you. How could you think that I wouldn't try to contact you?" His hands fisted beside him. "I laid in the burn unit for weeks and all I thought about, other than the pain, was you. I prayed you'd come back, that I'd open my eyes one morning and see you bending over my bed, feel your hand brushing the hair out of my eyes. But you never came. Not once."

Her throat tightened. "Colin, I didn't—"

"I came to see you. Did you know that? In Memphis, after I built this stupid house for you."

She blinked. "You built this house for *me*?"

"Every board of the wraparound porch I knew you'd love, the swing you've always wanted, the ginormous kitchen. Did you think I cared about having state-of-the-art appliances and an island? I can barely cook." He waved his hands in the air, as if waving away his words. "Doesn't matter. None of it. I went to Memphis to tell you about the house, use it as a bribe to try to get you to come back. But you'd moved on with someone else."

She stared at him, shocked. "I'd moved on? What are you talking about?"

"Your marriage. Obviously, it didn't last. You're not wearing a wedding ring and you sure haven't mentioned a husband since coming back. But you had no problem finding someone else. Your father told me all about it."

She took a step toward him, shaking her head, anger over this latest example of her father's lies tempered only by her grief and dismay. "And you believed him?"

He stared at her, confusion crinkling his brow. "You never got married?"

She clutched her hands together, tears burning the backs of her eyes. "No. I didn't."

This time, he took a hesitant step toward her. "You didn't…find someone else?"

"How could I? No one I've ever met compares to you." She slowly moved closer, then stopped. There was still far too much space between them, literally and figuratively. "I don't know what was going through my father's mind when he lied to both of us. He told me your burns weren't that serious, that you were released from the hospital that same day. And he forbade me from contacting you, said it would jeopardize my brother's trial, that he could end up in prison and it would be my fault."

Colin stared at her, but didn't say anything.

"Looking back, it's easy to see that it was foolish of me to believe him. But I was young, and naive, and terrified that I could be the reason my brother's life was ruined. That's hard to understand, I know. But back then, it was our family against yours. We were trying to keep Brian out of prison. You were going to testify against him. That's probably why Daddy kept the letters secret. He wouldn't have wanted me to read them and be conflicted between working to help Brian and being by your side."

She swallowed, hard. "I'd like to think that he felt guilty, that he realized he'd done both of us wrong by hiding your letters. That's the only reason that makes sense for him saving them all this time."

She took another step toward him. His intent gaze followed her as she slowly crossed the room.

"I read them in Memphis before I came back, half a dozen times. You were in so much physical pain, far more than I ever imagined. I had no idea how badly you were burned. I didn't even know you'd ended up in a burn unit. I'm surprised it wasn't mentioned during the trial."

He squeezed his eyes shut. "I didn't want to pile it on, to make things any worse for your family than it had to be. If Brian went to prison, I wanted it to be because of the arson, and almost killing two people, not for what he did to me. So we asked the prosecutor to keep the information about the severity of my injuries out of the trial. But I still thought you'd at least ask about me." He opened his eyes, raw pain staring back at her. "You never did."

"Oh, Colin," she whispered, her throat tight.

Six feet away, five. She stopped directly in front of him, so close that she could feel his heat reaching out to her.

"What do you want, Peyton? Is there even a point to this, now? If you can't stand the sight of me, there's no way we could ever heal the mistakes of our past." His voice was flat, his expression blank. But there was no hiding the warring emotions in his stormy eyes. There was pain, so much pain. Frustration, anger. And something…else. It was the something else that gave her courage. And hope.

"What I want is to explain my earlier reaction to seeing you without a shirt on."

His jaw flexed. "That's not necessary." He started to turn away, but she grabbed his arm.

"Wait." She dropped her hand. "Please."

He faced the doorjamb a moment, before turning back. "What?"

"The earlier letters, the handwriting wasn't yours. Who wrote them?"

He blew out a breath. "Duncan most of the time. Adam some of the time. Even Ian pitched in on one or two. My hands were bandaged. Everything was bandaged from my neck to my naval. I couldn't hold a pen."

Her heart squeezed in her chest. "You dictated the letters?"

He gave her a crisp nod and stared over the top of her head. "Is that all?"

"Later, the writing changed. It was messy, hard to read. That was you, wasn't it? In spite of the pain, the difficulty, you pushed through. Even though I never replied to your earlier letters. You kept writing."

"Oh for the love of…enough, Peyton. There's no reason to go through all of this. I was eighteen, nineteen by the time I was out of rehab and back home. Young, in love, in pain. But life goes on. Time passes. We grow up. Let's leave the past in the past."

"You still love me, Colin. That's not in the past."

He opened his mouth as if to protest, then closed it without saying anything.

"You love me," she repeated, knowing her heart would shatter if he denied it.

After an eternity, he finally replied. "Doesn't matter."

She let out a shaky relieved breath. "I love you too."

He stiffened, as if she'd hit him. "Doesn't. Matter."

"Why not?"

He laughed, but there was no humor to it. "We've both been fooling ourselves thinking that this, that you and I, could ever work out. Even if your brother didn't start the barn fire, he's guilty for the death of Officer Jennings. And I'm the one trying to put him back in prison. He's likely to face the death penalty. You'll never be able to forgive me for that, in spite of everything you've found out about him since coming back. And I couldn't blame you. I can't imagine being in your position. If something like that happened to one of my brothers, it would destroy me. So I'm okay with you not being able to forgive me. I understand. But it will always be there between us."

She shook her head. "There's nothing to forgive. Brian made his own choices. You're doing your job and what's right. I wouldn't be here trying to help you catch him if I didn't understand that."

He dropped his head to his chest before meeting her gaze once again. "The deck is stacked against us. I've been hoping, all this time, that I was wrong. That we could make this work. Somehow. But aside from everything I already mentioned, if my scars are a barrier between us, there's no hope. That's not something I can change. It's out of my hands."

"Oh, Colin. Sweet, wonderful Colin. That's what I've been trying to explain. You misunderstood, earlier. Disgust is *not* what I felt when I saw you without your shirt. And it isn't what I feel right now."

She stepped closer and pressed both of her palms against his chest. He flinched, but didn't pull away.

She slid her fingers to the top button of his shirt. He grabbed her hands.

"Peyton, don't. Seeing the scars across a room is one thing. Up close is far worse."

She looked up at him. "Let me. Please." When he didn't move, she added, "Trust me."

His brow furrowed. But he slowly dropped his hands to his sides.

She went back to work on the button, beneath his wary gaze.

"I didn't feel disgust." She slid the button free and gently pulled his shirt open a few inches. "I wasn't horrified." She opened another button. His shirt gapped a good six inches now, revealing a crisscross of puckered scars over an otherwise incredibly well-defined chest that would have made most men envious, most women hot. She was no exception.

Another button freed. More scar-covered muscles bared to her hungry gaze.

And her touch.

She leaned forward and pressed her mouth against a particularly savage-looking scar, and kissed him.

He jerked at the contact. "Peyton." His ragged whisper was a mixture of confusion and wonder.

She kissed him again, while freeing the remaining buttons. His pulse leaped in his throat and his skin heated at her touch. Her own pulse rushed in her ears. She slowly pulled his shirt completely open, then watched his face as she reached up to slide the material down his arms.

Once again, he stopped her, his hands pressing hers down on his shoulders. "This is madness." His voice was husky. "When I carried those people out of the barn, their clothes had melted onto their bodies. They were burned far worse than me. That's how my chest was burned, from their clothes pressing against mine. But I was wearing a short-sleeved shirt, which gave me some protection. But not my arms. There wasn't anything between their melted clothes and the skin on my arms as I carried them. Do you understand what I'm saying?"

"The scars on your arms are much worse than on your chest. I understand, Colin. And it doesn't change anything. Let me do this. Please."

He searched her eyes, then slowly dropped his hands and turned around so she could pull his shirt off his shoulders, apparently giving her a chance to change her mind before seeing the worst of the damage the fire had done. She wasn't changing her mind.

She bunched the fabric, then pulled it off and let it drop to the floor. His back was smooth and well defined, even sexier than she'd remembered, with only a few small white lines on the sides showing where the burns extended from the front.

Then he turned around.

She drew a sharp breath. "Oh, Colin."

He stiffened. "I knew this was a mistake." He grabbed for his shirt, but she put her foot on top of it. He looked up at her, his hand still clutching the fabric.

"You don't need to cover up," she told him. "Haven't you been listening? When I spoke just now, it was out of guilt and regret. The only disgust I feel is for myself. There's sorrow too, of course. When I see the scars, I see your pain, think about how much you suffered. I wish I could have somehow saved you from that pain. That's what you see in my face. That's what you hear in my voice. Shock, yes. Because even after reading your letters, I still had no idea just how badly you'd suffered. Now, seeing it for myself…" She shook her head. "I'm so sorry, Colin. Regardless of who is responsible, I'm so sorry that you were hurt. And I'm so, so sorry that I wasn't there when you needed me."

She very deliberately leaned down and kissed a shiny, puckered scar on his right biceps.

His breath caught.

She placed both her hands on his upper arms, then feathered her fingers across his skin.

He slowly straightened, leaving his shirt on the floor. She straightened with him, keeping her hands on his arms, smoothing her fingers up and down, across the peaks and valleys of the angry marks that were the result of so much damage, had caused so much pain.

Then she slid her hands across his shoulders, down his chest, following the dark line she remembered in her mind, even though it was no longer there to guide her hand. She continued down, down to where his jeans sagged below his naval, hanging low on his lean hips.

His eyes blazed at her, his nostrils flaring as if he was struggling to breathe. She wasn't in much better shape. Her heart pounded in her chest. Every nerve in her body sizzled, and all she'd done was slide her hands over his chest and abs. There was more to explore. So much more.

She reached for the button on his jeans.

He grabbed her hands. "Don't."

She frowned. "Why? I love you. I want—"

He shuddered. "So do I. Believe me, I *want*. But if you go any further, I won't be able to stop. I want you too much."

"Then don't stop. I don't want you to." She tugged her hands free from his and reversed direction, sliding them up his body and linking her fingers together behind his neck. "If you doubt me, feel my heart. It's racing. For you, Colin. That's what you do to me. Still. After all this time. After everything that's happened. My body still yearns for yours. I yearn for *you*."

She slid her hands down and splayed them once again across the pads of his chest. "These scars are your battle scars. They're medals of honor. What you did, going into that burning building not once, but twice to save two people you didn't even know..." She shook her head. "That's incredible. And I assure you, seeing the proof of your character isn't a turnoff in any way. It's a turn *on*. Because of what it means. Touch me, Colin. Feel the truth of what I'm telling you."

She didn't wait for him to make a move. Instead, she lifted his right hand and molded it against her breast. He groaned low in his throat, his fingers flexing against her, caressing, stroking. Her entire body flushed with heat.

"You feel my heart racing?" she whispered. "It's never raced like that for anyone but you."

He shuddered again and raised his hands to cup her cheeks, gently stroke his thumb across her lower lip. "We can't do this."

She blinked, the fog of passion thinning. "What? Why not?"

"Because I can't protect you. When I said few people

can see my scars without being repulsed, I meant it. *I don't have any protection.*"

She frowned, not understanding. He stared at her, waiting. Then she got it, her eyes flying open wide. She almost whimpered with frustration. "You don't have any condoms? Please tell me you're joking."

He shook his head. "I wish I were. I don't have any..." He straightened. "Hold that thought." He headed into the bedroom.

She followed, pausing in the doorway to see him open the nightstand by his bed. He rummaged inside, then slammed it shut.

"Where the hell did I—" He ran into the closet.

Peyton wrapped her arms around her waist, beginning to feel depressed and a bit silly for initiating something both of them wanted so very much, but might not be able to finish.

He stepped back into the bedroom, holding a small box in his hand.

She blinked. "I thought you didn't have any? Now I'm wondering why you do." She put her hands on her hips, jealousy riding her hard and fast. She'd never thought of him with anyone else before. It had never occurred to her, which was dumb considering how wonderful he was. Any woman should be thrilled to be with him. Still, knowing that he'd been with someone else sent a jolt of pain straight to her heart.

He stopped in front of her and tossed the box onto the nightstand. "Stop looking at me like that, Peyton. I didn't buy those. Duncan did. For you."

"Duncan? For me? I thought he was engaged to someone else."

He frowned. "That's not what I meant. He bought them for me and you, not him and you."

She grinned and slid her hands down his chest toward the top of his jeans. "I'm teasing. Be sure to thank him the next time you see him. For me." She winked and unbuttoned his jeans. "But we don't need them quite yet." She slowly, ever so slowly, unzipped his pants, her gaze locked on his. "I've missed you, Colin." She pushed his pants down his thighs.

"Peyton," he rasped, his body jerking against her hands.

"And I've really…" She closed her fingers around him and stroked.

He swore and jerked again.

She kissed the base of his throat, using both of her hands to caress and treasure the very essence of him. "I've really missed this." She grinned and slid down his body onto her knees.

Chapter Twenty-Two

Beeeep, beeeep, beeeep!

Peyton jerked awake beside Colin, both of them bolting upright in bed.

"What *is* that?" She covered her ears against the high-pitched shriek.

"Smoke alarm!" He threw the covers off and jumped from the bed, dragging on his jeans as he answered. Before Peyton could even blink the sleep from her eyes, he was shrugging into his shirt and racing out the door.

Her heart seemed to stutter in her chest. She jumped out of bed and yanked another of Colin's shirts from a hanger in his closet to cover her nakedness. Then she ran through the family room to the kitchen where the awful electronic shrieking was coming from. She stumbled to a halt by the island, realization dawning as Colin grabbed a smoking pan out of the oven and dumped it into the sink.

"Oh, no! My apple pie!"

She ran to the sink and turned the faucet on, running water over the stinking mess while he opened the back door. He swung it back and forth to draw fresh air into the room and try to clear the smoke out.

Peyton grabbed the dish towel off its hook and ran to the far corner of the room just below the shrieking smoke detector. She batted the towel at it, furiously trying to force the remaining smoke away.

"Give it to me, shorty." He winked to soften the insult as he yanked the dish towel from her and waved it back and forth beneath the alarm.

"I'll hold the door open." She ran to the door and mimicked Colin's earlier strategy, pulling the door back and forth to force air in and smoke out. The ceilings were high, compounding the problem of getting enough fresh air in to make the alarm stop even though most of the smoke had already cleared.

Finally, blessed silence reigned inside the house once again.

She looked back at him, wincing when his gaze met hers. "I completely forgot about the pie."

"That's okay." He grinned. "I thoroughly enjoyed making you forget."

Her face heated and he laughed.

He stepped to the sink, his nose wrinkling. "Give me a second. I'll toss this outside to get the smell out. I can bag it up in the morning if the wildlife doesn't take care of it by then." Using a couple of pot holders, he picked up the ruined pie pan and carried it to the door.

She moved backward, pushing the door open for him and stepping out to let him pass.

"Nice shirt. Definitely looks better on you than me." He winked, then froze, his gaze transfixed by something behind her. "My phone's on the nightstand by the bed. Call 911." He tossed the pie to the ground and grabbed his boots off the deck.

"What's wrong?" She whirled around, then covered her mouth in horror. The sky was glowing an eerie orange farther down the mountain. "The woods! They're on fire!"

He already had one boot on and yanked on the second. "Not the woods." His gaze met hers. "Your house. Go. Call 911."

She grabbed his arm. "Don't. It could be a trap."

"It probably is. But Landry has an officer stationed at your place to keep an eye on things. If Brian or your mom are there, the officer could be in serious trouble."

Her stomach lurched at the thought of the three escapees tied to a tree, burned alive. "Don't go. Please. It's too dangerous."

"I have to. Every second counts in a fire." He shrugged off her hand. "I'll use the ATV from my workshop. I can take a shortcut through the woods and get there faster than in my truck."

"What about your vest, your gun?"

"After what happened last time, I put backups of both in the workshop building. Go!" He leaped off the deck and took off.

Peyton ran inside the house, vaulted over the coffee table and practically flew toward the master bedroom.

This can't be happening. Not again. Dear Lord, please keep Colin safe! And please protect the officer at my house.

She was running so fast by the time she reached the bedroom that she couldn't stop. She fell against the bed then jerked upright and grabbed the phone, putting it on speaker mode so she could talk to the 911 operator as she yanked on her jeans and blouse. She rattled off the address while stuffing her feet into her sneakers.

Beeeep, beeeep, beeeep!

Peyton winced at the sound of the smoke alarm going off again. Had she forgotten to turn off the oven when she took out the ruined pie?

"Ma'am?" the 911 operator called out. "Are you still there? What's going on?"

Peyton blinked, her eyes burning. She couldn't see any smoke, but she could smell it. "I'm not sure. The smoke alarm is going off inside the house again."

"Again? Are there two houses on fire?"

That thought sent a cold chill down her spine. "I don't know. Just tell the firemen to hurry, please, to the Sterling house," she said. "That's where Deputy US Marshal Colin McKenzie went. Send the police too. Brian Sterling, an escaped convict, may be in the area. He may…he may have set the fire. His mother, Molly Sterling, could be with him." She coughed and looked around. Was the air getting thicker or was it her imagination? "Both are arsonists and extremely dangerous."

Beeeep, beeeep, beeeep!

The alarm seemed much louder now. No, all of the alarms in the house were shrieking now, not just the one in the kitchen. What was going on?

"I've got police and fire rescue on the way, ma'am. Please stay on the line until they arrive. Check those alarms, Miss Sterling. You might have to evacuate the house. If you do, stay outside and wait for the police to give you further instructions."

Peyton let out a disgusted sound. "That's not happening." She tossed the phone onto the bed and wiped her tearing eyes. She located his pistol and two magazines in the nightstand. She shoved a magazine into the gun, snapped the holster onto her hip and pocketed the extra magazine.

She looked through the bedroom doorway. The house was definitely getting smoky. But it didn't seem thick enough for the house to be on fire. And she didn't see any flames. Could it be that smoke from the house fire down the mountain was blowing this way and seeping inside, setting off the alarms? Maybe that had been the plan all along. Brian, or her mom, had set the Sterling house on fire to draw Colin outside.

If so, their plan was working.

She was about to run out of the bedroom when Colin's parting words echoed in her mind. He'd said he had an extra Kevlar vest in the workshop. Which meant the one he normally used should be in his closet. She ran inside and saw it hanging on hooks on the back wall, next to a rifle. She was wicked good with a rifle. Much better than with a pistol. And it would give her the ability to shoot from farther away. She didn't want to get in close and interfere with whatever strategy Colin might use. But if she could do something to protect him from afar, she absolutely would.

Thankfully Colin didn't take the same precautions of locking up his gun and ammo in his bedroom as he'd done in the pantry, probably because he wouldn't expect any guests to rummage through his bedroom closet. There was a box of ammunition on the top shelf, out in the open.

Rifle in hand, she ran out of the bedroom, coughing against the smoke. Then she swore and ran back in for Colin's truck keys. She grabbed them and took off toward the garage.

The smoke was worse in the garage, probably because it wasn't as airtight as the main house. She pressed the button on the wall to start the door rolling up and ran to the truck. As soon as she threw open the driver's side door, she swore a blue streak. How was she going to climb up into the stupid thing? There was a sports car on the other side of the garage. But she'd looked in the window before and saw that it was a stick. She'd never learned to drive a manual transmission.

Colin needs you.

She gritted her teeth, grabbed the steering wheel and tried to lift her leg inside. The stupid vest was so big and stiff it pushed against her thigh, making it impossible. She coughed again, then tossed her rifle into the truck and tore off the vest. After pitching it inside, she grabbed the steering wheel again and slung her right leg up. There! She had her foot on the door threshold. Now all she had to do was—

The passenger door flew open and her brother stood in the opening, aiming a pistol at her. "Don't even think about going for your gun."

Chapter Twenty-Three

Colin ducked down beneath the thick curtain of smoke in the living room of the Sterling house, holding a wet dish towel over his mouth to help him breathe.

"Officer? It's Marshal McKenzie. Can you hear me? Where are you?"

The only sound he heard was the roar of the flames licking across the walls. The only thing not burning was the floor, and that wouldn't hold true much longer.

No one had been outside when he got there. He'd run to the front of the house, confirming there was a patrol car in the driveway. But he hadn't found the officer to go with it. Knowing Brian and Molly, if they'd set the fire as a trap for him, the officer was probably inside. But even knowing that might be their plan, to roast him alive, he had to go in and try to find the missing officer.

"Hello? Is anyone in here?"

Nothing. He took a few more steps into the inferno, dread coiling in his stomach when he saw the hallway that led to the bedrooms. It was completely engulfed. If the police officer was back there, Colin was already too late.

He took another step, then another, squinting against

the dark smoke. Even crouching down with his nose and mouth covered, he could barely breathe. The heat and smoke were too intense. He had to get out of there. A blazing recliner forced him to move farther into the room and give it a wide berth so he could head back through the kitchen where he'd come in. He almost fell over the body that came into view. A uniformed officer was lying facedown.

He scooped the body up in his arms, the slight weight telling him it was likely a woman. But the smoke was so thick there was little else he could see. Eyes streaming tears, he threw her over his shoulder and sprinted toward the kitchen.

A loud crash sounded behind him as part of a wall caved in. He jumped to the side but a piece of wood slammed his shoulder, almost knocking him to the floor. He stumbled, using both hands now to clutch the officer while he held his breath. Whirling away from the burning cabinets in the kitchen, he ran out the door into the backyard.

He didn't stop running until he was far enough from the house not to feel the heat of the flames. Then he dropped to his knees and lowered his burden to the ground. Coughing and blinking against the sting of smoke, he used his shirtsleeves to wipe at his streaming eyes. When he could see clearly again, he bent over the officer to check on her. That's when he realized his mad dash into the house had been in vain. There was nothing he could do to help Officer Simmons. A bullet had blown away the back of her head.

He fisted his hands beside him and swore viciously. What a senseless loss of life. He lifted his head and scanned the woods behind the house. Where were the cowards who'd set this trap for him? Why weren't they laughing right now from the woods as Brian had done that night he'd cornered Colin by the workshop? Why weren't they shooting at him when they had him right where they wanted him?

Maybe they were behind him, waiting for him to turn around. He carefully drew his pistol, then jumped to his feet and whirled. Nothing. There was no one there. He turned in a slow circle. Then stopped. Orange flames danced against the distant night sky, right about where his house would be.

Right where he'd left Peyton while he raced down here to try to save someone else.

His heart lurched in his chest. He shoved his pistol into his holster and ran toward his ATV, parked twenty yards away.

Let her be okay. Please, God. Help me make it in time to save her.

He started the ATV, then took off up the mountain.

"I DON'T UNDERSTAND. Why are you doing this, Brian?"

Peyton stood outside of the workshop building watching Colin's dream house, their dream house, burn to the ground. Beside her, Brian stood watching the same thing. But where she was devastated, he was smiling, the flames from the house reflecting in his eyes, making him look every bit the devil that she now knew him to be.

"Brian? Where's Colin?"

He sighed and turned toward her, the pistol still in his hand, but pointing at the ground instead of her. She didn't kid herself into thinking it was because he didn't want to risk shooting her. He probably just didn't want to keep holding the heavy gun up in the air.

"I imagine he's at our house, the old Sterling homestead. He's too late though. It's a flaming mess by now. He won't be able to put it out."

"You imagine? Then you didn't hurt him?"

He gave her an aggravated look. "I've never killed anyone, Peyton, in spite of what your boyfriend has probably told you. He stole ten years off my life, would have stolen more if I hadn't escaped. All the other witnesses at the barn fire were kind of iffy, not a hundred percent certain it was me. They were easy to discredit. But McKenzie swore up and down he had zero doubt. It was his testimony that put me away. He ruined my life." He gestured toward the fire. "Now, I'm ruining his. Or, at least, as much as I can before I disappear. This is my revenge. Maybe sometime down the road, after he rebuilds, I'll pay him another visit. But for now, this will have to do."

He holstered his pistol. "I know you don't believe me. But I didn't set that barn fire. I didn't kill that cop, the one in Memphis. This fire—" he motioned toward the inferno in front of them "—is my first real fire. I have to admit, it's cool. I doubt it'll be my last. But just like I made sure you and McKenzie were out before I lit this one, that's what I'll always do. I'm not the evil person you think I am."

She tried to follow his twisted logic, but none of it made sense to her. "Then, you're just walking away? You came here tonight to burn Colin's house down?

And burned our family house down to get him out of the way?"

"Worked pretty good. There is one other thing." He pulled her to him and hugged her tight.

She stiffened and pushed against him.

He sighed and let her go, his eyes sad. "You were always there for me growing up. I told you at the high school that I'd never hurt you. I meant it. I'll never hurt you. Goodbye, sis."

He turned his back on her and started walking away. It was then that she noticed the ATV just past the corner of the workshop building, his getaway vehicle. She didn't try to stop him. She turned around and started jogging the other way, toward her old house. She had to get to Colin, to see if he really was okay. Or whether her brother was lying once again.

"Not so fast, Peyton."

She stumbled to a halt as two people stepped out of the woods across from her. Colin was in front, his clothes and face blackened with soot. The shirt he wore hung half open, some buttons torn off. He clearly wasn't wearing his Kevlar vest, and she didn't have to guess why. Her mother must have made him take it off. She was standing behind him, slightly off to the side and pointing a pistol.

"Mom?" she whispered, her voice breaking. Even though she'd already suspected that her mother might still be alive, seeing her had Peyton's whole body shaking. The woman looked twenty years older than she had almost four months ago. Her skin glowed a sickly yellow in the flickering light from the fire. Her once-blonde hair had turned almost white.

Part of Peyton wanted to run to her, to hug her and tell her how good it was to see her again. But the rest of her wanted to shake her mother and yank that gun out of her hand.

Colin's gaze was riveted on Peyton. He didn't seem to notice—or care—that his house was burning to the ground. He gave her a subtle nod, as if to let her know he was okay. Then he looked past her, off to the left, and his jaw tightened into a hard line.

She turned around to see her brother running up to them, a look of fury on his face. "Mom? What are you doing? You were supposed to let me handle this."

"Colin McKenzie is still alive," she said. "You haven't *handled* anything."

"I didn't come here to kill him. I did exactly what I wanted." He waved toward the house, which was crackling and roaring on the other side of the lawn. "We need to go before the firemen and cops get here."

"No. He destroyed your life, Brian. He deserves to be punished."

Peyton took a step forward. Colin frowned and shook his head, but she ignored him. She had to. She couldn't do nothing and risk her mother pulling the trigger. Somehow, Peyton had to turn the tables, get the advantage. She took another step, and her mother turned the gun. On Peyton.

"Oh, Mom," she whispered brokenly. "What are you doing? Why did you fake your death? And why would you destroy Brian's life by breaking him out of prison when he could have been a free man in a handful of years? If anyone has ruined his life, it's you."

Molly Sterling narrowed her eyes. "I'm dying,

daughter. I don't have much longer. And prison was killing your brother, not that you noticed. I told your father a few years ago during a visit with Brian that we needed to come up with a plan to get him out. That he wasn't going to make it to when his sentence was up. Your father called us both fools and refused to see his own son after that. So I had to take matters into my own hands."

Peyton took another step closer, then another. "How did faking your death help Brian? I don't understand."

Her mother rolled her eyes. "I was carjacked, back in Memphis." She snorted. "Can you imagine? Turned out to be a blessing. Some homeless-looking woman took my purse, my jewelry, then drove off in my car. She hadn't gone a block before the fool ran off the road into a tree." She laughed again, as if the woman's death was funny.

Peyton's stomach clenched with nausea.

"I was going to call the police, then stopped," her mother continued. "I realized what a boon this was. I could disappear and no one would come looking for me. The accident must have ruptured the fuel tank. The whole car reeked of gas. All I had to do was reach in the broken window and take my lighter from my purse, then…" She shrugged, a mad light dancing in her eyes.

"Oh Mom," Peyton whispered, nearly choking on her grief and disgust at what her mother had done.

"Disappearing allowed me to work on my plan to get Brian out. Your father was watching me too closely. He saw I was searching on the internet for information about prison transports and threatened to call the police if I didn't stop."

She smiled at Brian, who was staring at her a short distance from Peyton, his mouth open in horror. "I had to break my baby out. As soon as that stupid lawyer of his filed another one of his ridiculous motions to get Brian a break from prison, I made my move." She laughed. "A break. Ha. I broke him out, little old me. All it took was a bribe to an overworked, underpaid van driver to weaken the lock on the back of the van."

Brian stepped closer to Peyton. "Peyton's right, Mom. If you hadn't interfered, I'd have been out soon. But you had to shoot that cop. If they catch me now, I'm facing the death penalty just because I ran, because I chose to escape like the other guys. They'll never believe that I wasn't in on your plan, that I didn't know you'd be there, or that you'd shoot anyone. I'm guilty by association."

Peyton sucked in a breath. "Mom? You killed Officer Jennings?"

"A mother will do anything to save her son. Don't you see?" She looked at Brian, her eyes imploring him to understand. "You were wasting away behind bars. You know you wouldn't have made it until the end of your sentence. I had to get you out, see you freed before I died."

Colin suddenly spun around and yanked the pistol out of Peyton's mother's hand. He whirled back toward Brian just as Brian brought up his own gun and leveled it at Colin.

"Brian!" Peyton yelled. "Don't!"

Her mother stumbled back, then circled closer to Peyton's brother. "Shoot him, Brian. That's what we came here for. Shoot him."

"Like you shot Officer Simmons at the old Sterling homestead?" Colin asked. "You left the body inside to lure me into the inferno. Did you hope I'd be killed in the fire?"

Brian's eyes widened. "Mom? No. Please tell me you didn't do that."

Colin sidled toward Peyton, keeping his gun trained on Brian. But he stopped several yards away, probably to keep Brian's gun from pointing anywhere near her.

"How many people have you killed, Mrs. Sterling? There's Officer Jennings in Memphis, Officer Simmons, the three fugitives who escaped with Brian—"

"What?" Brian's eyes had gone even wider, his face losing all its color. "We tied them up so we could escape on our own, Mom. What did you do after I left to talk to Peyton?"

"The same thing she's done all along," Colin said. "Eliminated anyone who was an inconvenience. I'm guessing it all started with the sorority-house fire at your college, isn't that right Mrs. Sterling? What happened? Did one of the girls steal your boyfriend or something? So you decided to kill her?"

"What…what's he talking about?" Brian sounded confused, lost. His gun was still pointing at Colin, but he kept glancing at his mother.

Peyton clenched her hands at her sides, panic making her pulse rush in her ears. She was desperate to help but not sure what to do that wouldn't make things worse or get someone killed.

"Mom?" Brian asked again, his voice turning angry. "Is Colin telling the truth? You killed those men?"

"They don't matter," she said. "None of that matters."

Brian swore.

Peyton pressed a hand to her mouth, hot tears coursing down her cheeks. How had she never realized how twisted and evil her mother was?

Sirens sounded from down the mountain, just barely loud enough to be heard over the crackling of the fire.

"Drop your gun, Brian," Colin told him. "It's your only chance of getting out of here alive. Soon the mountains will be swarming with cops."

"Shoot him and let's go, before the cops get here," his mother urged.

Brian's gun wobbled.

"Don't, Brian," Peyton said. "I can't let you hurt him."

Colin frowned at her. "Stop it, Peyton," he whispered harshly.

He wanted to protect her. He obviously didn't want her trying anything. But these two screwed-up people in front of them were her family. She couldn't stand silently by while they discussed whether or not to kill the man she loved. She had to do something.

"I know you didn't start the barn fire, Brian," she said.

His wild-eyed gaze flicked to hers. "You're just saying that because you don't want me to shoot McKenzie."

"I don't want you to shoot him. You're right. I love him, very much. But I love you too. And I'm not lying when I tell you that I know you didn't torch the barn. I have proof, a picture. It shows mom inside the barn with the flames licking at the windows."

He frowned. "No way. I would have seen that picture at the trial."

"It's that smoking gun picture. We all looked at it a thousand times. But I looked at it again just a few days ago. And that's when I saw that forest-print fabric from Mom's dress in the lower edge of the window, just as the flames started. She was inside while you were taking the gas can out, thinking you were helping. She let you go to prison for her crimes. She didn't break you out of prison to see you free before she died. She broke you out to assuage her own guilt for letting you take the blame all these years. She didn't want to die with that guilt on her conscience."

Brian slowly turned his gun on his mother. "Is that true?"

His voice sounded so young, so bewildered and lost that it broke Peyton's heart.

Colin kept his gun trained on Peyton's brother. "Drop it, Brian."

"Mom?" Brian's voice cracked. "Mom?"

Her face crumpled, as if she'd finally realized that she'd lost the battle. Or was it all part of an act? Yet another lie to get what she wanted? "I'm sorry. I didn't know anyone was inside. And I didn't know you had run out with that can. I must have gone back in right after you ran out. If I'd known, I wouldn't have lit the match. I'm so sorry."

He slowly lowered his gun, a stricken look on his face. "You let me go to prison. All this time, you let me sit there, rotting away, when you were the one who should have been there."

Her mother sobbed, covering her face with her hands.

Brian turned his tortured gaze to Colin, then Peyton. "I wasn't in the woods that night, here, at the shooting.

It was Mom. She's the one who called Dad asking for money for both of us. I didn't know until later." He drew a ragged breath. "She gave me the gun for my protection in case the police were with you when I went to meet you at the school. It didn't bother her one bit that she handed her son the gun she'd used to kill his father." His tortured gaze met Peyton's. "She killed him. She killed Dad." He shook his head, tears streaming down his face.

Most of the sirens seemed to have stopped down the mountain, probably at the Sterling house. But one of them was still coming, probably a fire truck investigating the second set of flames lighting up the sky.

"Forgive me, baby," her mother pleaded, sidling closer to Brian. "You have to forgive me."

He ignored her, staring at Peyton. "I love you. I'm sorry, for all of this. But I can't go back to prison. I just can't."

She saw the intent in his eyes. "Brian, no!"

He jerked the gun up and shot himself. He dropped to the ground.

"Brian!" She started toward him.

"Peyton!" Colin yelled.

Everything seemed to happen as if in slow motion. Her mother threw herself to the ground, grabbing for Brian's pistol.

Peyton looked back at Colin.

He leaped toward her.

She twisted around to see her mother bringing up Brian's pistol and pointing it at her.

Boom!

Peyton was thrown to the ground, landing hard, her

chin snapping against the hard dirt. Colin had slammed into her, knocking her out of the way just as her mother had squeezed the trigger. She pushed herself up and looked back.

Colin was on the ground a few feet away where he'd landed and rolled, blood blooming on his side. His pistol had fallen out of his hand when he'd knocked Peyton down. She jerked her head up to see her mother smiling a sickening smile as she stared at Colin, Brian's gun still in her hands as she slowly aimed once more. This time, at Colin's head.

"Mom! Over here!" Peyton flailed her arms in the air.

Her mother jerked the gun toward Peyton.

Boom! Boom! Boom!

Her mother stared at her in shock, then slowly crumpled to the ground.

Peyton gasped, then whirled around. Colin lay on his side, his pistol in his hands where he'd snatched it up. Once again, he'd saved her. But at what cost? The dirt was soaked in blood beneath him. The pistol fell from his fingers and he collapsed onto his back.

"Colin!" She scrambled forward on her knees.

"Freeze! Don't move!" someone yelled behind her, and she realized the police had finally arrived.

She ignored them and hurried to Colin. He blinked up at her, as if having trouble focusing. The tears she'd thought had dried up flooded her eyes as she pressed her hand against his side, trying to staunch the flow of blood.

He gasped and gritted his teeth.

"I'm sorry. I'm sorry. I have to stop the bleeding.

Damn it, Colin. You should have shot my mother before she got Brian's gun back. Then she couldn't have hurt you."

He blinked up at her. "She's your mother. Didn't want you to hate me. Didn't want to shoot her."

"Oh, Colin. I could never hate you."

Rough hands grabbed her from behind. "Ma'am, back off."

"No, let me go! I have to put pressure on the wound."

Police were swarming across the yard, running toward them.

"Leave her alone," Colin rasped. "She's not one of the shooters. Leave her alone."

The policeman let her go and she scrambled to Colin's side, once again pressing against his wound.

"Get an ambulance," she yelled over her shoulder. "Marshal McKenzie has been shot."

"We're here," some EMTs yelled, scrambling toward them with their kits in their hands.

"Over here," one of the policemen shouted, waving at the EMTs as he knelt beside her mother. "This one's still alive. She's in rough shape."

"We've got another one over here," another policeman yelled. "GSW to the head, but he's still with us."

Peyton blinked. "Brian?" She saw the EMTs change direction and veer toward her brother and her mom. "No!" She glared at the EMTs. "McKenzie first. Get over here. Now!"

Another pair of EMTs seemed to materialize out of thin air and knelt beside Colin.

"Ma'am, please. You need to move out of the way and let us help him."

"He's bleeding. I can't move my hand. He's bleeding." Her tears ran down her face, dripping off her chin.

"I know, ma'am. We're going to help him. You need to let go."

"Peyton?"

She blinked furiously at her tears and looked down. "Colin?"

He lifted his hand and wiped at her tears. "I'm okay. I'll be okay. Let them do their job, sweetheart."

She blinked, then moved back, letting the EMTs take over. She scrambled around to his other side and stroked his hair as they put an oxygen mask over his face.

He lifted it up. "Don't cry, Peyton. They're working on your family. They'll do everything they can. Don't cry."

She pushed his hand away and put the mask over his nose and mouth. "I'm not crying for them, you silly man. I'm crying for you. You're my family. You always have been, always will be. I'm crying for you."

Chapter Twenty-Four

Peyton barely paid attention to the beautiful mountains and acres of green grass and trees surrounding them. She was too busy keeping a close watch on Colin since he insisted on driving the ATV. Even at a snail's pace, she could tell it was jarring his side, causing him pain. He was infuriating, refusing to follow doctor's orders and take it easy.

"If you rip out your stitches again, I'm going to let you bleed to death. Maybe then you'll finally learn your lesson and do what the doctor tells you to do."

"If you let me bleed to death, I won't be around to learn my lesson."

"Technicalities. Seriously, Colin. This is insane. It's only been three weeks since the shooting. The most *recent* shooting. Good grief. You've been shot twice in less than two months. You should be home in bed instead of driving me halfway across the mountain." She grimaced. "I mean at your parents' home, since *The Evil Ones* destroyed your beautiful house."

He gave her an admonishing look and steered around a fallen tree. "You need to quit calling your mom and brother *The Evil Ones*. They aren't evil.

They're…mentally unstable. They need our sympathy, not our scorn."

"Yes, well. You can give them sympathy. I'll give them scorn."

He smiled and shook his head. A few minutes later, he finally stopped the ATV. "Come on, my little protector," he teased. "Help me off this thing."

She hopped down and untied his crutches from the back. "You're not even supposed to be walking. Who gave you these things anyway? I don't see how they really help when you've been shot in the side. You should—"

He cupped his hand over her mouth. "Maybe you should take up baking again when you're rattled. My ears could use a rest."

She handed him the crutches and then put her hands on her hips. "Not funny. And I'm pretty sure I'm never baking again. It reminds me too much of my mother."

He eased down from the driver's seat and leaned on his crutches. "I heard she's doing surprisingly well, recovering from her gunshot wounds and responding to chemo and radiation. And there's hope for Brian too. The bullet lodged in his skull but they've managed to control the swelling. It's a miracle, really, that both of them are recovering so well."

She walked beside him, bending down to move sticks and rocks out of his way as he slowly ambled across the grass. "I wouldn't know. I haven't seen either of them."

He stopped.

She looked up at him, her brow furrowed. "Are you okay? Do you need me to bring the ATV over here so you can sit?"

"Why haven't you visited them? The trials are a long way off. You should take advantage of this time while they're both in the hospital and you can see them every day if you want."

She shook her head. "I chose you, Colin. I'll never make that mistake again. I'll always choose you."

He sighed heavily. "That's what I was afraid you'd say."

She frowned. "I don't understand."

He smoothed the hair back from her face. "I was wrong to ever say that to you, about choices. I was bitter, angry. I wanted you to put me first, before all others."

"I do. I will. I always should have."

He shook his head. "No. I mean, yes, we love each other. We should always look out for each other. But there's room in our lives for other people too. I never should have expected you to choose between me and your family. No matter what they'd done, no matter how sick or disturbed they may be, they're still your mother and brother. And I know that deep inside, you can't help but love them. I want you to know that it's okay to love them. And if you want to see them, I'm okay with it. I'll even go with you if you want."

Tears filled her eyes. "Dang it, Colin. You're making me cry again."

"I really do need to buy some stock in that tissue company you mentioned before."

She smiled through her tears. "You're such a good person. Far more forgiving than I think I'll ever be. But thank you. I'll think about it."

"That's all I ask. Now, I'd really appreciate it if you'd pay attention to your surroundings for a moment."

"I am."

He sighed and motioned with his head over her shoulder. "Not to me. To where we are. Turn around."

She did, then gasped. "Colin. It's...we're...oh my gosh. The beautiful meadow, and the mountains over there, and, oh, the waterfall. It's still pristine, so perfect. This is our secret spot, where we used to sneak off for hours in high school." She pointed to a spot near the waterfall. "That's where we first kissed."

"No. It isn't."

She frowned and turned back to him. "It isn't?"

He shook his head. "The first time we kissed was on the playground in second grade. You knocked me down and planted a big sloppy wet one right on my lips." He grinned. "That's the day I fell in love with you."

She blinked and wiped at a new flood of tears. "Oh, Colin. That's the sweetest thing. I didn't remember that."

"I remember every minute of my life with you."

"Tissues, dang it. I need a tissue." She swiped at her tears again.

"I'll kiss all your tears away in a minute. But there's one more thing you need to see. Turn around again. And this time, look down in the valley, on the other side of the waterfall."

She turned around. "What am I looking for, exactly?"

"Something orange."

"Orange? I don't..." She slowly turned back to face him. "Are those...property markers?"

"They're property stakes, yes. They mark the corners where the foundation of our new home is going to be built."

"Our new home?"

"I bought this land, our special place. And I want to build a future with you here, just like we always dreamed." He shifted one of his crutches and reached into his pocket, then held out a black velvet box toward her.

Her hands shook as she opened the lid. "That has to be the most beautiful thing I've ever seen."

"Not even close."

She glanced up at him in question.

"You," he said. "Nothing and no one is more beautiful than you."

She shook her head. "Those pain pills must be making you loopy. You're getting all mushy and silly."

"Then I must be doing this right." He shifted both crutches to one hand, and started to bend down.

She grabbed his arms, stopping him. "Don't you dare get down on one knee. I'll never be able to get you up again."

He grimaced and straightened. "You might be right. But I wanted this to be perfect for you."

She pulled the ring out of the box and handed it to him. "Just pop the question okay? That's all I need for this to be perfect."

He grinned. "Peyton Sterling, will you marry me?"

"Yes!" She was so excited she could barely hold still as he slid the ring onto her finger. She wiggled it in the sunlight, watching it sparkle. Then she threw her arms around his neck. "I love you, Colin McKenzie. More than you could ever know."

"And I love you, the future Mrs. McKenzie. Always have, always will."

"Would you just kiss me already?"

He was laughing as he pressed his lips to hers.

* * * * *

Look for the final installment of award-winning author Lena Diaz's The Mighty McKenzies miniseries, Undercover Rebel, *next month!*

And don't miss the previous books in the series:

Smoky Mountains Ranger
Smoky Mountains Special Agent

Available now from Harlequin Intrigue!

#1911 BEFORE HE VANISHED
A Winchester, Tennessee Thriller • by Debra Webb

Halle Lane's best friend disappeared twenty-five years ago, but when Liam Hart arrives in Winchester, Halle's certain he's the boy she once knew. As the pair investigates Liam's mysterious past, can they uncover the truth before a killer buries all evidence of the boy Halle once loved?

#1912 MYSTERIOUS ABDUCTION
A Badge of Honor Mystery • by Rita Herron

Cora Reeves's baby went missing in a fire five years ago, but she's convinced the child is still out there. When Sheriff Jacob Maverick takes on the cold case, new leads begin to appear—as well as new threats.

#1913 UNDERCOVER REBEL
The Mighty McKenzies Series • by Lena Diaz

Homeland Security agent Ian McKenzie has been working undercover to break up a human-trafficking ring, but when things go sideways, Shannon Murphy is suddenly caught in the crosshairs. Having only recently learned the truth about Ian, can Shannon trust him with her life?

#1914 SOUTH DAKOTA SHOWDOWN
A Badlands Cops Novel • by Nicole Helm

Sheriff Jamison Wyatt has spent his life helping his loved ones escape his father's ruthless gang. Yet when Liza Dean's sister finds herself caught in the gang's most horrifying crime yet, they'll have to infiltrate the crime syndicate and find her before it's too late.

#1915 PROTECTIVE OPERATION
A Stealth Novel • by Danica Winters

Shaye Geist and Chad Martin are both hiding from powerful enemies in the wilds of Montana, and when they find an abandoned baby, they must join forces. Can they keep themselves and the mysterious child safe—even as enemies close in on all sides?

#1916 CRIMINAL ALLIANCE
Texas Brothers of Company B • by Angi Morgan

There's an algorithm that could destroy Dallas, and only FBI operative Therese Ortis and Texas Ranger Wade Hamilton can find and stop it. But going undercover is always dangerous. Can they accomplish their goal before they're discovered?

_____

YOU CAN FIND MORE INFORMATION ON UPCOMING HARLEQUIN TITLES, FREE EXCERPTS AND MORE AT HARLEQUIN.COM.

HICNM0220

*Sheriff Jamison Wyatt has never forgotten Liza Dean,
the one who got away. But now she's back, and she needs
his help to find her sister. They'll have to infiltrate a crime
syndicate, but once they're on the inside, will they
be able to get back out?*

Read on for a sneak preview of
South Dakota Showdown *by Nicole Helm.*

Chapter One

Bonesteel, South Dakota, wasn't even a dot on most maps, which
was precisely why Jamison Wyatt enjoyed being its attached
officer. Though he was officially a deputy with the Valiant County
Sheriff's Department, as attached officer his patrol focused on
Bonesteel and its small number of residents.

One of six brothers, he wasn't the only Wyatt who acted as an
officer of the law—but he was the only man who'd signed up for
the job of protecting Bonesteel.

He'd grown up in the dangerous, unforgiving world of a biker
gang run by his father. The Sons of the Badlands were a cutthroat
group who'd been wreaking havoc on the small communities of
South Dakota—just like this one—for decades.

Luckily, Jamison had spent the first five years of his life on his
grandmother's ranch before his mother had fully given in to Ace
Wyatt and moved them into the fold of the nomadic biker gang.

Through tenacity and grit Jamison had held on to a belief in
right and wrong that his grandmother had instilled in him in those
early years. When his mother had given birth to son after son on the
inside of the Sons, Jamison had known he would get them out—
and he had, one by one—and escape to their grandmother's ranch
situated at the very edge of Valiant County.

It was Jamison's rough childhood in the gang and the immense responsibility he'd placed on himself to get his brothers away from it that had shaped him into a man who took everything perhaps a shade too seriously. Or so his brothers said.

Jamison had no regrets on that score. Seriousness kept people safe. He was old enough now to enjoy the relative quiet of patrolling a small town like Bonesteel. He had no desire to see lawbreaking. He'd seen enough. But he had a deep, abiding desire to make sure everything was right.

So it was odd to be faced with a clear B and E just a quarter past nine at night on the nearly deserted streets. Maybe if it had been the general store or gas station, he might have understood. But the figure was trying to break into his small office attached to city hall.

It was bold and ridiculous enough to be moderately amusing. Probably a drunk, he thought. Maybe the…woman—yes, it appeared to be a woman—was drunk and looking to sleep it off.

When he did get calls, they were often alcohol related and mostly harmless, as this appeared to be.

Since Jamison was finishing up his normal last patrol for the night, he was on foot. He walked slowly over, keeping his steps light and his body in the shadows. The streets were quiet, having long since been rolled up for the night.

Still, the woman worked on his doorknob. If she was drunk, she was awfully steady for one. Either way, she didn't look to pose much of a threat.

He stepped out of the shadow. "Typically people who break and enter are better at picking a lock."

The woman stopped what she was doing—but she hadn't jumped or shrieked or even stumbled. She just stilled.

Don't miss
South Dakota Showdown *by Nicole Helm,*
available March 2020 wherever
Harlequin Intrigue books and ebooks are sold.

Harlequin.com

Get 4 FREE REWARDS!

We'll send you 2 FREE Books plus 2 FREE Mystery Gifts.

Harlequin Intrigue books are action-packed stories that will keep you on the edge of your seat. Solve the crime and deliver justice at all costs.

FREE Value Over $20